Praise for (

Family Secrets

'A heart warming and realistic s
put it down. Ideal book for 12+.'   Melissa

'True to life – very emotional' Lydia aged 12

'I believe that Family Secrets is a brilliant book and that it
shows a lot of emotion.' Aiden aged 12

'Family Secrets is a really imaginative and eventful book. It's
absolutely great for teenagers. Especially because of the
emotions and how realistic the characters are! Jade yr7

'I think Family Secrets really inspired never to get upset
about bullies and never punch them in the nose.' Joseph
aged 11

'Awesome book, great storyline. I didn't put it down from
start to finish.' Megan aged 18

'Family Secrets' named book of the week June 2010 by
Rotherham Library Service.

Family Fear

'This is an enthralling storyline and the way the writer
captures the personality of the characters is amazing. Once
I started reading I couldn't put the book down.' Christina –
12-year-old bookworm!

'A great read. Inspiring and heart warming with the
occasional disaster! A real page turner, highly
recommended!' Naomi (adult)

'An excellent follow up to 'Family Secrets'. Once I started
reading 'Family Fear' I could not put it down until it was
finished. Pam (adult)

To my mum – love you loads!

To Pam for all you do and for the special friend you are.

And to all the children and young people I've worked with at Sunday Special and Friday Club. I've enjoyed every minute of it and still do!

CHAPTER ONE

"Gran?"

Searching the tidy bungalow, I knew something was wrong. It was like, over an hour since Gran left the old person's centre, she should've been here ages ago.

"Gran, are you here?" Only silence answered me.

"Aargh!"

A sharp rap at the front door exploded into the silence. Walking down the hall, I could make out two dark shadows through the frosted glass on the door. I took a deep breath to try and calm down then reached for the handle, my hand shaking. Opening the door, I sucked in air, then couldn't seem to breathe out again. Two uniformed police officers stood there looking really grim.

"Rachel Brooks?" The male officer asked.

"Yes?" My voice quivered, my fingers gripping the door handle so tight it was like they were welded to it.

The female officer smiled, weakly.

"May we come in?" She asked, as ice crept over my heart.

"What's it about?"

"We would rather discuss that inside." The male officer's voice was firm.

I wanted to shut the door, pretend they weren't there, turn around and find Gran in the kitchen. But instead, I stepped back and opened the door wider, hardly daring to breathe. It felt really weird, like I wasn't really there, just watching the TV or something as they stepped past me into the hall.

Leading them into Gran's sitting room, I perched on the edge of the settee and scowled as the male officer settled into Gran's chair.

"Rachel," the female officer sat down beside me, "It's about your grandmother ..."

***

Only the day before I'd looked out through rain streaked windows, watching the familiar Scarborough landscape, grey and wet, come into view. So much had changed since I left five months ago. Back then I thought I was Rachel Brooks, fifteen years old, daughter of Janet and Michael Brooks, an only child. Now I knew the only real part of that was my age. I could still see the look of smug satisfaction on evil Emma's face when she ruined my life, telling me I was adopted. I closed my eyes, trying to block out her image, but it was no good, she was still there behind my eyelids. Opening them again, I gazed out of the coach window and wished we'd never moved away from Scarborough.

Rain lashed the glass as the engine shuddered then fell silent and I saw him. Of all the people I'd have loved to see after being away, Joshua Green wasn't one of them. I mean, like, what was he doing hanging around under the trees in West Square in the pouring rain?

I joined the line of disembarking passengers and climbed down, trying to stay out of sight as I followed the driver around the back of the coach. I shivered as cold rain splashed down, seeping through my hair and running down my neck.

"Is this one yours?" The doubled up driver asked as he heaved my red suitcase from the depth of trunk.

"Yeah, thanks."

Extending the handle, I trundled it behind me away from the coach and Joshua Green.

"Whoa, Rachel Brooks!"

Stopping abruptly, my stomach tightened, I forced a smile before turning to face the eighteen-year-old nightmare.

"Hello, Joshua."

Rain ran from his short black hair down his face and neck, but he didn't seem to notice as he smirked, hungrily.

"So, what brings you back here? You miss me too much?"

I wanted to spew.

"I've come to visit Gran."

"So, how is the old girl?"

"Fine."

"Well, maybe we can get together while you're here."

'*Not if I have anything to do with it*' shot through my mind but, "Erm, I'm gonna be real busy with Gran, I haven't seen her for ages." Is what I actually said. Swiping away my damp fringe, I shivered again. "Look, Joshua, I've got to go, I'm getting soaked."

"Yeah right, see you around. I'll be watching out for you."

I really was gonna spew.

"Bye." My smile was weak as I hurried away. Icy water splashed from scattered puddles into my trainers, but I didn't care, the rain had given me a good excuse to escape creepy Joshua.

With squelching feet, I almost ran along the damp streets, with my head down and shoulders hunched. I couldn't wait to see Gran's welcoming bungalow with ivy and roses growing up over the walls and around the door.

Finally I turned a corner and there it was. There was a whole line of white prefab bungalows but Gran's was the only one I really saw. She's been living there for years and the ivy she'd planted had nearly covered the whole of the outside.

I really was running now, down the street and through the open wooden gate into Gran's small rectangular garden. It only took three strides to reach the brown front door. A quick knock and I was in.

"Is that you, Rachel?" The familiar voice called from the warmth inside, as I shook off the wet in her narrow hall.

Dragging my suitcase inside I called, "Yes, Gran, it's me. But you ought to keep the door locked, you know."

Tutting, she emerged from the sitting room on my right.

"If I had locked the door, you wouldn't have been able to get in, now, would you? You would still be standing outside in that awful rain instead of drying off in my hallway."

Gran hadn't changed. She was still short but sturdy, as Mum called it. She still wore her salt and pepper hair (more salt than pepper these days) in curls made by rollers and a perm. Her cheeks were still round and rosy and her blue eyes shone with love and fun behind her round, brown glasses. She was a real old fashioned kind of gran, like you see on the TV. She was pretty old when she had Mum, so Gran was really like, getting on a bit now.

10

A lovely warm feeling spread from my heart, right through my body.

"I've missed you, Gran!" Suddenly I was rushing forwards, throwing my arms around her and hugging her tight.

"Oh! How wet you are!" She cried, pushing me away and pulling her thick grey cardigan tightly around her.

"Sorry, Gran." Letting go, I grinned, gazing down into her familiar, loved face. "I really have missed you."

"I could tell by all those long wordy telephone calls and letters."

My cheeks burned. "Sorry, Gran, I meant to write but with all that happened ... I wish we'd never moved."

"Ah, now, I know you've had a hard time of it, but it was long past time for the truth to come out. I just wish it had happened in a better way for you, Sweetheart." Reaching up to rub my shoulder, her eyes suddenly twinkled with mischief. "But I do hear there is a good side to it all."

"Oh yeah?" I teased.

"You know what I'm talking about." Gran nudged me and winked. "A certain young man who goes by the name of Luke Chambers."

Even his name made tingles run around my stomach and up my spine.

"A real hunk, so I understand?" Gran raised her eyebrows, "Tasty is he?"

"Gran!" My cheeks burned. I couldn't have this conversation with my gran, my mates yes, but Gran?

"Well now, get those wet clothes off and tell me all about him!" She said, giving me a push towards the small guest room at the back of the bungalow. "I'll want to know every detail mind and all about your new twin, Rebecca too!"

I was still shaking my head as I went into the bedroom. Gran could be *so* wicked.

The guest room hadn't changed at all. The same cream lamp and old wind up clock stood on the oak dressing table. Gran's red jewellery box and crystal dish filled with potpourri decorated the oak chest of drawers, each standing on its own home-made cream crocheted mat. I smiled, remembering when Gran tried to teach me to crochet; totally bad idea. I was hopeless. I got the wool so tangled up that Gran had to cut it to get my fingers free! She never tried to teach me again after that!

I dragged my case over to the wardrobe but couldn't be bothered unpacking, I just unzipped it and dragged out a clean pair of jeans and blue top. Flinging them onto the patchwork duvet, I walked over to the dressing table and grimaced when I saw my reflection. Talk about wrecked! My brown hair, normally fine and wavy now looked like a drenched mop on my head. My mascara had run so much, I looked like something out of a horror movie with long black streaks running down my cheeks. Thank goodness my lipstick was waterproof otherwise I'd look like a vampire who'd just fed.

I stripped off my soggy coat. My pink top and jeans were so wet I looked like a wet T-shirt contestant which was *soooo* not a good look for me. My 'curves' were like, bigger than they should be and the clingy look was definitely not for me!

Anyway, I repaired the damage and ten minutes later, I sat with my legs curled up under me on the soft sofa in Gran's sitting room. Gran sat opposite rocking gently in her old wooden rocking chair. The suite was the old fashioned kind with dark wooden arms but comfy cushions. Cupboards made of the same dark wood, lined the walls. On each one sat crocheted white doilies with little girl ornaments and fancy photo frames. No matter where I looked pictures of Mum, Dad and me smiled out into the room.

I felt much better sitting in warm, dry clothes, drinking tea and spilling my guts about all the rotten things that'd happened since we moved away.

"Nasty piece of work that Emma Samuals, friends with you one minute and the next turning on you just because a boy she liked smiled at you. Why ever did you make friends with her in the first place? Surely there are better girls than her in Rotherham? And how did she find out you were adopted when you didn't even know yourself?" Gran stopped rocking and looked at me with a little frown.

I shrugged. "She was the first person who was nice to me after we moved. I like, thought she was so good at first, sticking up for me against the bully, Carly Thompson on my first day at school. I didn't find out what a psycho she is until it was too late. Her dad's a reporter and he recognised my dad when he collected me from their house one day. Emma's a real snoop and she listened in on her parents when her dad told her mum all about me. She loved telling me about it in front of everybody. I hate her. "

Putting my mug down on the mahogany coffee table, I slipped my thumb to my mouth and began chewing the nail, a habit I'd caught from Becca, my only friend, other than Luke at school. I often wished my twin, Rebecca went to the same school, at least then there'd be four of us against the rest.

"It must have been hard, Sweetheart. I never did agree with your parents' decision not to tell you about your adoption. I know they felt guilty about not adopting Rebecca but your mum could hardly know that one year after you were abandoned another little bairne would be found, could she? It broke my Janet's heart not adopting her, but her cancer was so bad at the time …"

"I know, Gran, I've tried to tell them it's okay but it's like they can't forgive themselves so don't think I'll forgive them either. Not telling me the truth was worse than them not being able to adopt Rebecca."

Gran tutted and shook her head. "How are things at home now?"

"Weird. Everybody's watching every word. It's like we're all scared we'll say the wrong thing and upset everything again. I mean, we're getting on better now, but like, everything's changed and we're not really sure how to talk to each other any more. To be honest Gran, I couldn't wait for the summer hols., so I could come see you and get out of their way for a bit. I need a few weeks when I can just chill and forget about everything."

"You should have called me, Love, when it was all going on, I could have helped you."

"I know, Gran. But I didn't want to drag you into it. Mum and Dad were so defensive and dead against me searching for Rebecca, I didn't want them having a go at you too. Anyway I sorted it on my own."

"With a little help from your lover boy!" Gran said, her eyes twinkling.

"Gran!"

A sharp knock at the front door saved me. I heard it open, than a fraction of a second later the sitting room door burst open. We both jumped and Gran clutched her chest.

14

"Rach! You're here!" Sam entered like a whirlwind, her dark face alight, eyes glowing and slim body alive with exaggerated actions.

"Now then! You nearly gave me a heart attack, Samantha Wintoga!" Gran frowned up at my best friend.

"Oh, sorry, Mrs Banks, I was just so pumped about seeing, Rachel." Sam's many tight black plaits bounced as she spoke.

"Well, you'd better come in now, but take off that coat, you're dripping all over my lovely carpet."

"Oh sorry, Mrs Banks." Sam dodged back into the hall, stripped off her coat and dropped it onto the floor.

Gran tutted. "There are coat pegs out there, Samantha."

"Oh, yeah, sorry." Sam reached down, retrieved the coat and hung it by its sleeve on the opposite wall. My grin grew. It was so good to be back.

"So ..." Sam bounced back into the room and flung herself down beside me on the settee, "How's it feel being back in Scarborough?"

"Like I never left, even down to creepy Joshua sniffing around," I said, wrinkling my nose.

Sam grinned. "Girl, some things never change."

"Creepy Joshua?" Gran raised her eyebrows.

"Yeah, you remember, Mrs Banks, he's a real idiot. He was always following Rachel around when she lived here," said Sam, not noticing my warning glare.

"Oh, dear," Gran said, frowning. "Rachel, I didn't know anything about this boy, perhaps coming back without your parents wasn't such a good idea after all. I don't like the sound of this Joshua. Perhaps you would be safer in Rotherham?"

15

"No, Gran!" I shot a panicked and pointed look at Sam, then pleaded with Gran. "I'm all right here. I want to spend some time with you. And anyway, I need some space from Mum and Dad. I'm not worried about Joshua, you know how Sam exaggerates."

"Oh, yeah, you know me Mrs B.," Sam said, picking up on my silent instructions, "You know how my mouth flaps. Rach'll be fine. Anyway, I'm here, I'll look after her."

Gran looked doubtful, but the worried frown melted.

"Very well, but you tell me straight away if that boy gives you any trouble. You hear me, now?"

"Sure, Gran," I said, knowing I wouldn't. Gran was such a worrier she'd have me on a coach back to Rotherham faster than I could blink.

Thankfully she believed me and relaxed back into her chair.

"So, Rachel, what are your plans, now you're here?"

"I'm gonna spend as much time with you as I can, Gran and basically just chill out." Just saying it made me feel better.

"Now, you don't want to be spending all your time with an old girl like me. You need to spend time with people your own age, catch up with your friends, like Samantha, here."

"You're not old, Gran and it's you I came to see."

"Oh, thanks!" Sam's hands shot to her hips as she made an unconvincing attempt to look miffed.

"You know what I mean." I gave Sam a 'behave yourself' look.

"And I know what you mean too," Gran said, "So, I will make you a deal. You both challenge me to a game of scrabble. After that you can both skidaddle and give an old girl some peace to have a nice nap. Deal?"

"You're on!" Jumping up, I headed straight for Grandma's old bureau. The tall china filled display cabinets on either side stood like guards on sentry duty beside the writing bureau and three drawers beneath. "Is it still in the second drawer, Gran?"

"Of course."

Fishing out the worn box, I headed back to the settee. It was gonna be fun. Playing scrabble with Gran was never dull.

***

"I can't believe some of the words your gran came up with." Sam shook her head making her thin plaits toss like one of those bead door curtains Gran used on hot days.

"Well, I reckon she's got a good imagination," I said, grinning as we walked through town two hours later.

"Imagination, I'll say! Wasabee! I mean!"

I laughed. I could still see Gran's fake wounded look when we told her it wasn't a word.

"Oh, yes it is," she said. "It's what you call a dead bee, it wasabee."

Like, sure.

"And then there was Zebho, right on a triple word score!" Sam ranted.

I smirked. "What did she say that was?"

"She said it was a cross between a zebra and a horse. And when we challenged her on it, she said that today's education system was 'obviously sadly lacking'! As if!"

"She's fantastic."

"She can't spell."

"She does it on purpose."

Sam stopped walking. "What?"

"Yeah, didn't you notice? Whenever she tried one of her words she stuck her tongue in her cheek."

"I never noticed that!"

"Well, that's what she does."

"But you let her get away with it!"

"Yeah, I know." I grinned.

Sam shook her head. "I don't believe you. You let her off with all those words. She thrashed us!"

"Yep."

Smiling, I gazed around at the familiar shops, the Brunswick Shopping Centre, Sulman's Gifts and Dash as we walked down Westborough then turned towards the cliff lift.

"Remind me why we're going the long way around instead of straight down to the front," Sam said, ogling a six foot hunk as he walked past.

"Because I want to walk all along the sea front," I answered. "I haven't seen it in ages!"

"It's only been five months! What do you think's changed in that time?"

"Nothing, I hope." My heart was sort of aching, like I was gonna see an old friend.

When we reached the cliff lift, I pulled Sam away to the left.

"Let's walk down the path. I want to see all the view."

"Walk down!" Sam cried. "You've got to be off your head. It's freezing and windy enough to blow us right off! The last people will see of us is our feet flying over their heads as we're whisked away!"

She was right. It was a wild day. The waves on the high tide were huge and covered in white foam as they crashed onto the beach. I shivered, it might have stopped raining but it was still cold.

"Go *on*, Sam," I urged, breathing in the salty air as it stung my face. Seaside air has its own smell, its own taste.

Sam rolled her eyes. "First day back and you're gonna have us freeze to death." She shook her head. "Okay, let's go, but you owe me one."

We set off down the winding path, Sam muttering as we walked.

"It's supposed to be summer but the weather thinks it's the middle of ruddy winter. We should be sat down there on the beach with bikinis and ice creams not shivering in our flipping coats!"

Sam gave a great shudder and pulled her coat around her, just to let me know she meant it.

"Oh, no, look who's coming." I'd been looking down at the harbour and the lighthouse when movement caught my eye. Just two lengths of the path away was Joshua with three of his friends.

"Told you we should have used the lift. Come on, let's go." Sam caught my arm and tried to pull me back up the path.

"No, I'm not gonna hide from Joshua for the next four weeks. No way!"

"Hey, Rach!"

I instantly changed my mind, wishing I'd listened to Sam.

"Hello, Joshua." My voice was flat.

"So, I thought you were with your gran?" His eyes scanned down me then slowly climbed back up. It made me feel sick.

19

"I have been but she's having a rest now so I'm gonna meet my mates."

"How about we come with you?" His hands swept out to include his friends. He licked his lips. "We'd liven your afternoon up."

I tried to look apologetic.

"Sorry, Joshua, I've not seen them for ages, we've got a lot of girl talk to catch up on."

"Okay, this time," Joshua's voice deepened, making me shiver. "But I won't let you keep putting me off."

His smile did nothing to take away the feeling I'd just been threatened.

"See you around." Joshua had one last hungry scan over me then passed us and walked away up the path.

My spine quivered like a spider had crawled up it.

"You want to stay well out of his way, Rach." Sam warned, linking her arm into mine. "He's trouble."

"I know." I shivered again, but this time it wasn't because of the cold. "He always was."

"No, I mean, real trouble. You've probably not heard. His dad found his mum with another man, or so the rumours say, so his dad walked out."

"When?"

"Not long after you left. Since then he's been done for shoplifting a couple of times. Ruby says he's been drinking loads more since he left school and his temper's got worse with it. I heard he hit a girl at a night club the other week just because she wouldn't dance with him. You've really got to stay right away from him."

"Don't worry, I'm gonna," I said, my face set as I marched down the path. "I'll avoid him like the measles."

"Trouble is, sometimes measles get you anyway ...," said Sam.

CHAPTER TWO

"Hey, Rach!" Ruby's red head popped up from the people milling around the entrance to Luna Park, a wide grin stretched across her round freckled face.

"Ruby!" I waved like a three-year-old and walked faster. "Hey!"

Now this was really like coming home. In Rotherham I'd been like an ant in a school of anteaters but these were my real friends.

"Yo, Rach. How's it feel being home again?" That was Summer, smiling all over her sun-tanned face. Summer was one of those rare blondes who didn't burn but just turned a fantastic shade of brown. She was short for her age too, a bit smaller than me so I didn't feel like such a shrimp around her.

"It feels great!" I said, grinning like a kid in a toy shop. Standing below the ferris wheel its multi-coloured baskets swinging, with the sound of slot machines, seagulls and music from the rides filling the air felt wonderful. "I just wish it was for ever."

"Yeah, Sam told us what happened to you." Summer frowned. "I couldn't believe it when I heard about your adoption and everything. You must've been totally freaked, like, how do you handle somethin' like that? And that Emma idiot, where does she get off?"

I rolled my eyes. "I know, just because she thought I was hitting on Luke she turned into this, like, total psycho and I hadn't done anything! Well, not then, anyway." I smirked. "That came later."

"Justice!" We all shouted together.

"So, about Luke. Is he a good kisser?" That was Ruby.

My cheeks burned, Ruby could always do that to me.

"Yeah," I said, "He's a good kisser. He's got these gorgeous blue eyes and he's a total hotty!" I sighed, my spine tingling at just the thought of his arms around me. "I never thought I'd end up with somebody as fit as Luke."

"Pity you didn't bring him with you." Summer looked like she was gonna drool.

"Well, looking at you, I'm glad I didn't. He's mine, so hands off!"

"Hey, Rachel, what's Rebecca like?" A soft voice spoke out from behind Ruby and a tiny head peeked out.

"Hey, Sapphire, I didn't see you there."

Sapphire was Ruby's younger sister by two years and they were like, as different as sun and snow. Sapphire was quiet, shy and tiny with the most brilliant blue eyes you could ever see. Ruby was noisy, outgoing and well, large.

All eyes turned to me, Ruby leaned forward, her eyes sparking, "Yeah, Rach, what's this twin of yours like?"

I chewed my lip.

"Well, you know what she looks like," I began.

"No, we don't," said Summer

"Duh!" Ruby gave her a shove. "They're like, identical twins! What's she supposed to look like?"

Summer frowned.

I grinned. "Well, her face is sort of, round like mine, with this funny turned up nose. I hate my nose," I said, pointing at it. "And her hair's the same colour, but hers is shorter. She's a bit thinner than me as well."

I liked ice cream and KFC too much, not to mention pizza. Sam always says my bumps are in the right places but I think she seriously needs glasses. "Oh, and she's dead blunt, always says what she thinks."

"Ruby'd like her then. Ow!" yelped Sam, when Ruby thumped her on the arm.

"So, do you see much of her?" Summer asked.

I shrugged. "Some. We're getting to know each other a bit but it's not been easy with homework and seeing Luke as well. She only lives about six miles away though so she comes over when she can."

"How hard was it to find her?" Sapphire's quiet voice asked.

I groaned. "Real hard. There were like, so many dead ends. If it wasn't for this news editor with Social Services connections tipping me off with her adoptive parents' names I don't think I would have managed it. But once I'd got them the internet did the rest."

"Are you still trying to find your birth parents?" Summer asked, changing the subject.

I shrugged. "I dunno. Not right now but I might in the future. It's like I don't really know who I am until I find them, y' know?"

"Yeah, it must be real weird not knowing where you come from," said Summer.

"Yeah, I mean the aliens might still be looking for you. Their mother ship might be above us right now." That was Sam.

I rolled my eyes.

"Yeah, sure, you reckon." I'd had enough of the spotlight for now. "Look, I don't know about you lot but I'm about ready for a ride on the dodgems. How about it?"

"Yeah." Sapphire's eyes sparkled.

"I'm gonna thrash you all!" I said, grinning.

"You're on!" Ruby and Sam echoed together.

Sam slung her arm around my shoulders and we marched off, past the water spray games and the arcade with clattering coins. We waited for the dodgems to stop then nearly took over the next round with all of us in separate cars. Our aim was definitely NOT to avoid each other! As soon as the music started we all floored the peddles and aimed straight for each other. My head jerked forward then back as my car hit Sam's head on then I was flung to the left as Sapphire's car slammed into the side of mine. Ruby crashed into Sapphire and Summer smashed into Sam. We were all laughing as our engines roared, each of us trying to unsuccessfully twist away but we were going nowhere. The rest of the riders were left to try and drive around us. In the end the attendant came over and moved Sam and me away. The others were then free and set off after us. They cornered me at the edge of the ring and whacked right into me. My car spun around and I raced off again.

By the end of our session I'd definitely NOT thrashed the others. They'd all ganged up and crashed into me from all sides. I scrambled out of the little purple car feeling like one big bruise and my neck could have used a brace.

"You bullies!" I said, pretending to look angry.

"Well, we'd got some time to make up for. You were seriously owed some bashing," Summer said. The others nodded.

"Oh, thanks," I groaned. "I think I'll go back to Rotherham, at least I get beaten up by my enemies there, not my friends."

"That's not what we heard," said Ruby, "Is it Sam?"

"Nope," Sam shook her head. "Rach did her own share of bashing."

25

"Only when I had to!" I protested.

We hung out for the rest of the afternoon, walking across the sand in our bare feet, trying to push each other into the freezing sea. Later we sat on the low sea wall, our backs resting against the black railings, eating hot dogs and catching up with news before finally stuffing our faces with ice creams.

"I don't know about you but I'm frozen!" Sam shivered violently.

I grinned. "Yeah, I think those ice creams were a big mistake."

"You don't say!" Ruby's voice oozed sarcasm. She was the only one who hadn't been crazy enough to eat one.

My fingers were like ice and I slipped my hands into my coat pockets.

"I think it's time I got back to Gran's and spent some time with her. I'm gonna get in front of her fire and warm up a bit! See you all tomorrow!"

"Yeah, okay," agreed Summer, "My tea's calling. Hope it's spag. boll. I could just eat some spaghetti."

We all rode up in the cliff lift together then called our goodbyes and set off in different directions. I went out of my way to walk a bit further with Sam and finally said 'Goodbye' on Gladstone Road where she turned right and I turned left towards Gran's.

"See you tomorrow!" I shouted. She gave me a 'royal wave' over her right shoulder and a quick wiggle of her bottom. Grinning I set off towards Wykeham Street then nearly jumped out of my trainers when Joshua stepped out of Norwood Street, straight in front of me.

"Joshua!" I gasped. He stood right in front of me, a longing leer all over his ugly face.

26

"Hey, Rach, nice smile, you glad to see me or somethin'?"

My skin prickled like ants were crawling all over it.

"Oh, hi, Joshua. No, well, I was thinking about my friends. I'm meeting them just down here," I gabbled.

"Really?" His crooked grin looked too confident. "So, you didn't really mean it when you said goodbye to them all at the cliff lift? Except Sam, of course, who's up there." He pointed to where Sam was just disappearing into Rothbury Street.

I clenched my jaw, wishing she was nearer, so I could shout for help.

I shivered and turned back to Joshua, frowning.

"You were following me?"

His grin spread wider. I swallowed.

"Look, I've got to get to Gran's."

I tried to side step around him, but he stepped at the same time blocking my way. My eyes flicked around, hoping to see somebody nearby but it was tea time and there was only an old couple way up by Tindall Street. My heart beat harder, I could feel it thumping against my ribs as Joshua stepped closer.

"I've missed you, Rachel." His eyes looked like a cat eyeing a bird as they slid down my body.

I could see my jacket moving in rhyme with my pounding heart.

"Look, I'm sorry, Joshua, but I've really got to go."

I tried to side step again, on the inside this time, but he blocked me again, stepping right up to me, his chest almost touching mine. His breath smelled of alcohol. It tickled my cheek, making me want to shrink away. His right arm came up onto my waist. My

27

stomach lurched and I stepped backwards. My back pressed against the wall and Joshua stepped in. I was trapped.

"You and me, we'd be good together," he said, breathily, stroking his hand up and down my side. "I've allus fancied you, but you were too boring before. You've changed. I could see it as soon as you got off that bus. Maybe you should've found out you were adopted years ago, you'd have been more interesting." His rubbing became firmer, his left hand coming up too. I could hardly breathe.

"Let go, Joshua," I croaked. "I've got a boyfriend."

His grip tightened, his fingers digging in. Then they relaxed and the stroking began again on both sides now.

I was frozen, like I'd turned to stone.

"But your boyfriend isn't here and I am." His head came down, his warm breath on my neck sending shivers all through me. "What he doesn't know won't hurt him. I could show you a real good time, Babe." His hands lifted up the edge of my T-shirt and slipped underneath as his wet lips touched my neck. Instinct took over. My right knee jerked up with as much force as I could manage and crunched between his legs.

"Aargh!" he cried, dropping back and bending double, his grip released.

For an instant I stood, my eyes wide in shock, watching him, his hands dropping to hold himself. I couldn't believe what I'd done.

'He's gonna kill me!' The thought shot into my mind and I ran. I raced along the street like I'd never run before. What had I done? I was supposed to be avoiding him, but instead, I'd like, kneed him in the groin! He'd murder me once he recovered. I'd just

reached the corner of Wykeham Street when his shout, full of hate, made my blood freeze.

"You'll pay for this, Brooks! Just you wait, you're gonna PAY!"

CHAPTER THREE

By the time I reached Gran's I was like, totally out of breath, my lungs felt like they'd explode. I was shaking from the ends of my hair to the tips of my big toes. It wasn't until I stood on the pavement outside Gran's bungalow that I dared look back. I scanned the street, standing on tiptoe to see over parked cars then sagged with relief when there was no sign of Joshua.

I leaned against the fence trying to calm down and get my breath back. I couldn't let Gran know what'd happened or she'd have me on the first bus back to Rotherham. It wasn't like I hadn't settled in there or anything like that, I *mean*, Luke's there! It's just that Scarborough still felt more like home and, you know, I wanted time with Gran and my mates. I just couldn't go back yet.

After about five minutes I could breathe better and only my hands were still shaking a bit. I figured I could finally go in without Gran seeing there was anything wrong. I walked to the door and tried the handle but it was locked. Reaching up, I rang the bell, grateful that Gran had finally got some sense. Within a minute of the sing song chime, Gran's blue outline appeared behind the frosted glass. I heard the chain rattle and the key turn in the lock. Then the door opened a tiny fraction and Gran peeped out.

"It's me, Gran," I said, my voice still wobbly.

"Ah, Rachel." Gran closed the door and I heard the chain rattle again. "Come on in, Love."

"Thanks, Gran."

I stepped inside and Gran frowned up at me, her eyes peering above her glasses.

"Are you all right, Sweetheart?"

"Yeah, I'm fine." I tried to sound happy and light hearted.

"Are you sure, Love? You don't sound all right."

That was Gran, as sharp as a needle, she knew me better than anybody else. I thought fast.

"Yeah, Gran, I'm okay, I just rushed home because it's getting really cold and, you know, seeing everybody again ..."

I let Gran fill in the blanks and thankfully she did.

"Aw, Sweetheart, you have missed them all haven't you? Never mind, you have four whole weeks to spend with them now."

I put on my best smile.

"I know, it's okay. So Gran, what's for tea?" A wonderful smell had been wafting down the hall towards me from the second I walked through the door. My mum's a good cook but Gran's awesome. She still cooks her own chips instead of going to the chippy and they were always big, fat, soft and juicy. "Chips?"

"Your favourite, chips and hash. Come, get cleaned up and I'll serve."

As I followed Gran down the hall, the incident with Joshua replayed in my mind. Maybe I'd got it wrong, maybe he just got carried away and didn't mean anything. But I kneed him in the groin and no matter what his intentions, now I'd done that, he definitely meant that threat!

***

31

Later that night, I sat cross legged on my bed in my soft pink dressing gown with a bath towel wrapped around my wet hair like a turban. Gran had gone to bed half hour earlier so it was safe to ring Sam without being heard.

"Hey, Sam," I whispered when she answered.

"Hiya!" Her voice boomed into my ear.

"Shhh!"

"Why? What's up? I'm not that loud, I'm on the other end of the blooming phone!"

"Shhh!" I hissed again, "Gran might be old but her ears are dead sharp. I bet she'd hear somebody sneeze three streets away. If she wakes up and hears me on the phone she'll tune in and I don't want her to hear what I'm saying, okay?"

"Yeah, okay. Wow, must be juicy then," Sam said, a bit quieter. I could picture her chocolate face expectant, like a dog eyeing up a bone. "Go on then, shoot. What's up?"

"I bumped into Joshua on my way home."

"I told you to avoid him."

"He came out of a side street right in front of me, what was I supposed to do, disappear?"

"Now who's being noisy?" Sam chirped back. I bit my lip realising she was right. "So, what happened?"

I told her everything, right up to me running off and Joshua yelling after me.

"Woa, that is so, not good." Sam's voice was suddenly serious.

"What am I gonna do, Sam? He's gonna kill me." I clung to the phone, needing a good answer, a way out of the mess.

"You've got me." I could almost see Sam shaking her head. "I mean, he's gonna be after your blood."

"Oh, thanks, cheer me up, why don't you? Come on, Sam, think of something. There's got to be a way out of this."

"I don't know. Look, you'll have to give me time to get my head around it. Just, stay out of his way, okay? Don't go anywhere near him. If you see him, run and I'll try and work something out."

"But what if I bump into him like today?"

"Don't."

"But what if I do?"

"Then run like your backside's on fire and don't look back."

Somehow that didn't really make me feel any better and I spent the night roaming around my bed like it was full of needles. When I did finally fall asleep I dreamt about Joshua chasing me around Scarborough. No matter where I ran he jumped out in front of me and grabbed me.

I was absolutely exhausted when I got up the next morning. My eyes were so black it looked like I'd been punched. I had to put on so much make-up, I could've used a trowel.

Tuesday was Gran's afternoon at the old folks' centre so we decided to spend the morning together. I was itching to talk to Sam but it would have to wait until Gran went to the centre. The rain and damp had finally gone, instead the sun was shining and it was actually warm. We set out together, Gran in a flowery dress and crocheted pink cardigan and me in my trainers, jeans and white T-shirt. I slipped a thin black jacket over the top.

Gran was pretty fit for her age and we walked for ages around the shops.

"I love these gift shops," I said, picking up a duck ornament made of shells. I'd lived in Scarborough since I was two years old but I still loved the gift and trinket shops. I used to spend hours in them as a kid, just wandering around, wide eyed, picking up all the little shell ornaments, nodding dogs, key rings and cuddly toys. I'd got a huge collection of them still waiting to be unpacked in Rotherham.

By 12 o'clock we were both exhausted. We found the nearest cafe and sank down at the first empty table. I dropped our bags at our feet and sighed.

"I'm shattered. You've worn me out, Gran!" I grinned at her and she winked back.

"There's life in the old girl yet!"

"There sure is, Gran. What're you having?"

Gran ordered ham sandwiches and apple pie. I had a jacket potato filled with prawns.

"You know, when I was young I had hollow legs."

Blinking, I looked at Gran, imagining legs with no bones, muscles or nerves inside. Like, how'd she stand up?

Gran must have read my 'easy to read' face (as Luke calls it) because she grinned and explained.

"It's just a saying, Dear. People say you have hollow legs if you can eat as much as you want and never put on an ounce in weight."

"Ooh." Some of my brain cells lit up and started functioning. "I wish. I've only to look at food and I put weight on."

Gran frowned. "You're not fat."

"I've got bumps where I don't want them. I watch what I eat, most of the time and I exercise but it's not working."

"Nonsense, you have a lovely figure. Yours is the Marilyn Monroe look, curvy."

"Fat."

"Curvy!" Gran's voice was firm and I knew not to argue.

"How's your mum going on with her writing?" Gran asked, spooning up a big piece of cream covered apple pie.

I shrugged. "She's had loads of rejection letters, she's real disappointed, but she won't give up. She just keeps sending it back out again."

"Now that's my Janet, never gives up. Well hopefully she'll get her novel published one day."

I wasn't listening. A movement at the window had made me look up. Joshua stood on the pavement outside, staring in at me, his eyes narrow and glaring. I gasped and stopped breathing. All sound faded except the beating of my heart. Joshua turned and came in. The bell jangled as he sat down at the nearest table opposite me. His eyes were like tractor beams, pulling me in. I forced myself to look away, to breathe and focus on Gran but he was still there in the corner of my vision. I could feel his eyes on me, piercing like lazers. Gran was talking but I couldn't hear her. What did he want? What was he gonna do? Why couldn't he just leave me alone? He was never like this when I lived here before.

There was another movement, I tried not to look but couldn't stop myself. Joshua's right hand was moving slowly across his throat from left to right, forefinger outstretched. Then with a wicked grin he slowly stood and left. I watched him walk past the window his eyes fixed on mine until the wall obscured him. I sat frozen in my seat, hardly breathing. I was dead, that's what he meant. I guessed he wouldn't actually kill me, but I knew I'd been threatened and whatever he'd got planned, it wasn't good.

I had to talk to Sam, she knew him better than me now. She'd know what to do. I half stood.

"Rachel? What's the matter? Rachel?" Gran's voice filtered into my malfunctioning mind and I like, came to my senses, like a spell had been broken or something.

"Er, yeah, er sorry, Gran." I sat back down, dragging my gaze away from the window and back to her.

"What's the matter, Sweetheart? Are you all right?"

"Er, yeah, Gran, I'm fine." I forced myself to smile and tried to think of a reasonable explanation for my weird behaviour. "Er, I was just thinking we'd better not be long or you'll be late for the Centre."

Gran glanced at her watch. "Oh, my, yes, how time flies. Well, we'd better drink up and be on our way."

I walked Gran to the old people's centre, then rang for a taxi. After dropping our shopping off at the bungalow I headed down to Peasholm Park where I'd arranged to meet Sam.

Within half hour we were in the front seats of an ugly green dragon boat peddling like crazy around the lake. I figured that was one place no one could hear us talk and it'd work off some calories.

"So he just sat there and made the cut throat sign?" Sam stared across at me like I'd said Victoria Beckham was fat or something.

"Yeah. Like he was trying to psyche me out. What am I gonna do, Sam? I'm here for the next four weeks. How am I gonna avoid him all that time?"

"There's no way you can." Sam sighed then yelled. "Hey, watch out for the island!"

I'd been looking at Sam and forgotten I was supposed to be steering. I snapped my vision forward as Sam yanked the steering wheel to the left. But she was too late.

There was a crunching, scraping sound as the side of the boat ground along the bank.

A seagull cried just above us and I could swear it was laughing at me. I scowled up at it.

"Well, thanks for the heart attack!" Sam said, holding her chest.

"It wasn't that bad."

"Bad enough. I think I'd better steer now."

I shrugged, "Whatever." And let go of the white steering wheel on the divide between us.

"So, no brilliant ideas then?" I asked, watching Sam with her tongue sticking out like steering took loads of concentration.

"Nope," she said, manoeuvring around a red dragon with a mum and dad in front, gran and screaming toddler in back. "But I'll get my wonder brain on the job and I'll come up with something."

But by the time we headed back to the landing stage she still hadn't thought of anything.

"Oh, no." The flat bridge behind the brown and yellow boat house came into view and my mouth went dry.

Sam followed my eyes.

"Oh great. That's all we need," she groaned. "What's he doing here?"

Joshua Green leaned against the wooden rails, his hands in his jeans' pockets, watching our boat approaching. Although his body looked really laid back, his face wasn't. His lips were pressed into a thin line, his eyes fixed on me, filled with anger, but, sort of, hungry and longing as well.

I wanted to head back out onto the water but the attendant was signaling us in.

My heart beat fast and loud, thundering against my ribs. As I climbed out of the boat my legs felt weak and wobbly, like the bones had been taken out. I didn't know how much of that was tiredness from peddling and how much was fear.

Joshua didn't move, he just watched me walk towards him. The bridge was divided by a metal fence down the middle, one side for those going onto the boats and the other for those unloading. Joshua was on our side. I wished there was another way I could go, but other than jumping into the water and swimming to dry land, the bridge was my only option.

I heard Sam scramble out behind me and my heart tripped a quick thanks when I felt her hand brush mine. She was walking so close it was like our arms were attached.

"So, Rach." Joshua's eyes fixed on mine. I looked down, but then this sudden surge of anger rushed through me like fire and I thought, 'Like, why should I let him intimidate me?' I shot my eyes back up and fixed them on his.

"What do you want, Joshua?" I said in the fiercest voice I could manage. Even I was impressed by how firm it sounded.

"Lose the sidekick." He nodded towards Sam.

"In your dreams," Sam growled.

"She stays," I said, my voice deep, hiding my panic.

Two young girls rushed past on the other side of the bridge, squealing in excitement.

"Hold on, you two! Calm down now or we won't be going on the boat," their mother yelled after them, a big holdall in each hand. Their dad followed behind running a hand through his non-existent hair.

Joshua waited until the family had poured into a boat and set off across the lake with a steady churning of water and more screams from the girls.

He pushed off the railings and stepped towards me. I automatically stepped back.

He stepped forward again and I made myself stand my ground although all I really wanted to do was run. I was so grateful to feel Sam at my side.

"So, Rach, I suppose you think you're tough now?"

I just stared at him. I didn't really know what to say.

"I knew you'd changed. You've turned into a right little scrapper. You're more like me than you think."

"I'm nothing like you!" I spat.

His eyebrows raised. "You think? Look, if anybody else did what you did they wouldn't be able to stand up right now. But, I'm gonna give you one last chance. Forget that no brainer of a boyfriend of yours and show me a good time while you're here. You do that and I might forget your little 'mistake'. But if you don't ..."

He left me to fill in the rest but I preferred to leave it blank.

"What a charmer," said Sam, her voice laced with sarcasm, while I shivered on the inside. I felt like a cold hand had just slid down my spine.

"Shut it, Wintoga," Josh hissed.

"Get lost Joshua, she'd never go out with you even if you were the last idiot on the planet."

I shut my eyes and thought. *'Nice Sam, that'll really smooth things over - not!'*

"You'd better shut your face or I'll sort you out as well!" Josh spat out, jabbing his finger at Sam.

I felt Sam stiffen and step forwards.

"Oh, yeah? I'd like to see you try, you ..."

"Shut up, Sam," I snapped, surprising myself as much as Sam.

"Yeah, Sam, shut up," Joshua said, smirking.

"You as well, Joshua!"

It was like somebody had taken all the fear out of my body and I was ready to fight. I was just so sick of being threatened, first Thompson, then Emma and now Joshua. I stood straight, the jelly gone from my legs.

"My boyfriend is not a no brainer, you don't even know him. I'm not cheating on him with you, not now, not ever. Just get lost and leave me alone."

I expected Joshua to explode but instead his wicked grin just spread, his eyes sparkling with evil. He reminded me so much of Emma when she told me I was adopted, that my new found courage instantly disappeared. My back sagged and my knees threatened to give way.

Joshua stepped closer and spoke, his voice deep and controlled. "Are you really sure about that, Brooks?"

I tried hard to swallow. I nodded, my reply blocked by the tightness in my throat.

Joshua leaned down, his breath brushing my ear, his words acid.

"Then you're gonna regret this, Brooks. Nobody does what you did and gets away with it."

Then he spun around his trainers squealing on the wooden landing and marched off without looking back.

"This is not good," Sam said, quietly. "It is *so* not good."

CHAPTER FOUR

My legs were so wobbly, Sam helped me to a bench. We sat, facing the water, watching others pedal their red and green dragons around the lake. I was shaking all over and couldn't stop. The sun was hot but I felt cold. I pulled my jacket tighter around me, wrapping it round like I was protecting myself from more than the cold.

"So what're you gonna do?" Sam asked after a few minutes.

I shook my head. "I don't know. Look, I know he's a creep, but he's not vicious. Is he?"

Sam shrugged. "I don't know. You've known him as long as me."

"Yeah, but you said he's changed since he left school. You said he's got worse."

Sam sucked in air slowly then bit her lip.

"Well, he has ... oh, I don't know. To have it in for you just because you won't go out with him... I don't know whether he's got that bad."

"It's not just that, is it? I kneed him where it hurts."

I stared out across the water. A little girl in a pretty summer dress stood in front of her mum throwing bread to a hoard of ducks. More ducks flew in, splash landing on the water, then waddling out onto the grass. Why me? Why did my life have to be so complicated? I mean, hadn't I been through enough this last few months? What with moving away, finding out I was adopted, dealing with evil Emma and being ostracised at school. Wasn't it my turn for a break?

Things should've been fantastic back here in Scarborough where everything was great before I left. What had I done to deserve all this mess?

***

It took a good half hour before I'd calmed down enough to think rationally. I walked around the park talking everything out with Sam, until eventually my feet went on strike. I flopped down on a bench and watched the red and yellow pagoda bandstand bobbing on the water with pigeons nestling on top. Lots of old folk sat on the raised seats facing it like they were expecting a concert any minute.

"What time is it?" We both checked our watches and I gasped. "I didn't know it was that late. Gran will have been home ages. She was gonna get tea for five. I'd better go"

As we walked I pulled my mobile from my bag to let Gran know I'd be late. It rang and rang. Eventually I pressed the 'end call' button, frowning.

"There's no answer."

"She's probably in the bathroom or out in the garden," Sam suggested.

"Yeah," I said, even though an uneasy feeling had already settled into the back of my mind. I walked faster.

On Gladstone Road I said goodbye to Sam and continued on alone. I tried ringing again and still there was no answer.

"Where are you, Gran?" I hissed and started to run. The anxious feeling spread through me, images of her laying on the floor of her bungalow, having collapsed or fallen pushed into my imagination and I ran faster.

At five thirty Gran's bungalow finally came into sight. With one final push of energy I ran to it, crashed through the gate and tried the handle. It was locked.

Reaching in my bag, I pulled out the spare key Gran had given me the night before.

"Gran?" I stepped into the hallway, listening for movement. "Gran, are you there?"

Only silence answered me. A cold hand grabbed hold of my heart and squeezed. I should still have been gasping for breath, but instead I could hardly breathe. I longed to hear Gran's cheerful 'hello'.

A search of the bungalow came up with nothing and I'd just decided to ring the day centre when a sudden hammering on the front door exploded into the silence.

I jumped and spun around, staring at the two dark figures through the frosted glass. I froze, something told me this was bad, very bad.

The hammering sounded again, setting my heart pounding in rhythm. I walked slowly to the door, my hand shaking as I reached out and turned the handle.

"Miss Brooks?"

I definitely wasn't breathing now as I stared at the two uniformed officers blocking my view of the road.

"May we come in?" The female officer looked full of sympathy.

Somehow I managed to lead them into Gran's neat sitting room, but glared at the male officer when he settled into Gran's rocking chair. He shouldn't sit there, only Gran sat there, it was like she was already gone. A lump jumped into my throat, I swallowed hard but it wouldn't go. My eyes burned and I blinked hard.

'Hold it together. Don't give in. Not yet. Maybe it's not that bad,' my brain ordered, but the lump wasn't listening, it was getting bigger.

'Just tell me!' I wanted to shout. *'Get it over with!'*

But then I changed my mind, I didn't want to know. I wanted them to disappear, to be gone and not come back. I wanted Gran to walk through the door a big smile on her face.

"Rachel." The female officer leaned into me on the settee. "My name is WPc Williams and this is Pc Mercer. We are here about your grandmother, I'm afraid there has been some trouble."

My heart beat so loud I could hardly hear her.

"I'm afraid she's been mugged."

Mugged. Not dead. Or maybe that was coming next. An image of Gran laying on the pavement, hurt, flashed into my mind and I bit my bottom lip to keep it still.

"She's been taken to hospital. We've come to take you to her."

This wasn't happening, it just wasn't happening.

"Is she ... Is she all right?" Stupid question, if she was all right she wouldn't have been taken to hospital.

"She was conscious when they took her in the ambulance, she asked us to come get you." WPc Williams spoke softly, trying to sound reassuring but it wasn't working.

"Was she hurt bad?"

"She is a little bruised and shaken. We'll take you to see her and the doctors will tell you more."

The officers stood, I looked around thinking I should take something with me. What do you take when you visit somebody in hospital? What do I need?

45

What does Gran need? The only thing that sprang into my mind was grapes, everybody took grapes to the hospital, but Gran hates grapes.

Officer Williams put her hand gently on my shoulder.

"Shall we put together a few of your Gran's things, a night gown, dressing gown, some soap, a flannel maybe?"

'She's not coming home then, Gran's not coming home tonight.' My eyes stung so badly I could hardly see. I blinked like mad and a tear squeezed out. I swiped it away. I had to think, what would Gran want? I went into her beautiful bedroom biting my lip really hard. I went over to her dressing table, its large mirror gleaming. Gran's cheval set sat proudly in the middle, a wedding present, she said, from my granddad. I ran my fingers over the shiny silver patterns on the brush, comb and hand mirror. Gran loved this set, used it every day, but she wouldn't want it in hospital in case it got stolen, I'd need to find another comb. The dressing table was covered with framed portraits of Mum, Dad and me. I picked up a black and white picture of Gran in her white wedding gown, Granddad stood beside her in his dark suit both framed in a church doorway, beaming smiles on their faces. They looked so young. My throat was so tight now I could hardly swallow. I put the picture down and forced myself back to work. Opening the top drawer, I found some clean underwear, a pretty blue night gown and some hankies. I pulled a clean cotton dressing gown from the wardrobe and picked up Gran's slippers. Then I collected her soap, flannel and toothbrush from the bathroom. What else? I gazed around and my eyes settled on Gran's makeup bag, she'd want her lipstick, Gran never went anywhere without her lipstick. I picked up the whole bag and a

46

comb from the side of the sink and took everything back to the bedroom. I found a little overnight case at the bottom of Gran's wardrobe and stuffed everything inside.

Once back in the hallway Pc Mercer took the case from me and WPc Williams handed me my shoulder bag. They led the way outside and Officer Williams took my key from me. She locked the door then put her hand on my shoulder, guiding me to the waiting police car. There was no sound, it was like I was in a bubble, none of this was real, I was gonna wake up soon, I had to.

But I didn't. The engine roared and the car pulled out. Gran's bungalow slipped away into the distance.

CHAPTER FIVE

As we drove along Woodlands Drive, I kept my eyes fixed on the back of Pc Mercer's head. He had a bald patch forming. I wondered if he knew.

"We're here," said WPc Williams, opening the front passenger door.

I didn't move. Gran was inside this hospital, hurt. I didn't want to find out what'd happened to her. She should be well and happy at home, not here. I tried to swallow but my throat was dry. I couldn't handle this. For the first time in ages, I wanted my mum.

WPc Williams obviously got tired of waiting for me. She came around to my side and opened the door.

"Come on, Rachel."

I swung my legs over the sill and climbed out. My stomach felt like it was full of cement as I looked up at the Main Entrance with its yellowish overhang. I followed WPc Williams in through the glass doors, trying not to look at the ambulances parked on each side of the entrance. Two blocks of chairs, their occupants sporting cuts, bruises and pained looks made my heart pound on my ribs like it was trying to break out. I stared down at my feet, my hands clenched so tight the nails dug into my palms as we walked to the reception desk. A toddler screamed like she was in agony. I wanted to stick my fingers in my ears. My stomach heaved. I clamped my lips together, trying not to be sick.

"Your gran's been taken to the ward. Do you want to follow me?"

I nodded, I was like, in emotional overload. I wanted to get out of reception and see Gran, but I was scared too. What if Gran was real bad? I trailed behind Officer Williams as she walked quickly along identical corridors. I'd no idea where we were going or how I'd find my way back. I remember seeing a sign for Xray and us riding in a lift, but it was like I was a zombie or something.

We finally reached a busy ward. WPc Williams walked straight in, but I spotted a hand cleanser on the wall and squirted some on my hands. I wasn't going to do anything to make my gran worse.

Hurrying, I caught up with the officer as she said, "Thank you," to a nurse in white tunic and blue trousers.

"Your Gran's down here." The officer turned to go, then stopped and looked down at me. "Are you all right?"

No, I wasn't, no way was I all right, but I just nodded. She didn't look convinced but still set off down the ward anyway. I kept my eyes on her back, not wanting to see all the sick people in the bays we passed. WPc Williams turned into the last bay. It had four beds but couldn't be the right place, none of these frail old ladies was my gran, they all looked so old and worn out. WPc Williams strode ahead and stopped by the second bed on the right. I looked at the tiny, pale old lady with a huge black eye and my lunch came up into my throat. I swallowed hard, blinking away stinging tears. It was my gran, wearing a pink night gown that hung loosely from her small body. She looked defeated and lost in the white sheets, propped up on pillows.

Gran's eyes were closed, the left one looked like it wouldn't open at all it was so black, purple and swollen. There was a cut above her right eye and her left wrist laying on the sheet was encased in a bright white pot.

"Gran," I whispered and walked right to her side. "Gran?"

The right eye flickered open and Gran's face brightened, but there was something missing. The spark, you know, the fire, the life. Her eye was dull, almost like the real Gran wasn't inside there anymore.

"Gran, are you okay?"

"Oh, Rachel." Her voice quivered as she reached out with her right arm and grabbed my hand. Her grip was so strong it felt like she'd crush my fingers. Her eyes watered and tears even squeezed out of the almost shut left eye.

My chest tightened like it was being squeezed by a gladiator. I'd never seen Gran cry before.

"It's all right, Gran." I managed to croak through the tiny straw that was my throat. "I'm here."

"Oh, Rachel, it was awful. He just came from nowhere and knocked me over." Gran's voice cracked and I couldn't stop tears escaping down my cheeks. "He tried to grab my bag, but I held on to it. Then he hit me so hard I was sure my eye would burst. He took my bag, I couldn't stop him." Her one good eye peered into mine like she was pleading with me to make things right and safe again. "What are things coming to when an old lady can't walk down the street anymore?"

"Mrs Banks, can you describe the boy who attacked you?"

I'd forgotten WPc Williams was there.

Gran shook her head, then screwed her face in pain.

"No. No, I can't."

50

"Do you think you would recognise him if you saw him again?"

"No."

I frowned, something was wrong. Gran's answers were too quick, she was lying, I was sure of it. But why?

"Can you tell me fully what happened?"

WPc Williams stepped around the other side of the bed and looked down on Gran. She held a notebook in her hand and leaned forward in a reassuring kind of way.

"It was just like I told Rachel."

"But, how was your wrist broken, was it when you fell?"

"Must have been. I don't remember." Gran shook her head again, more slowly this time.

I looked from Gran to the officer. WPc Williams knew Gran was lying too, it was written all over her face, from the raised eyebrows to the narrow lips.

"Very well, Mrs Banks. I'll leave my card with your granddaughter and she can ring me should you remember anything else." She turned to me. "Your grandmother's bag is on the floor just there." She pointed to the end of Gran's bed. I'd never even noticed her carrying it. "Do you have someone to stay with you?"

I stared at her, I'd not had time to think about being on my own at Gran's.

"I asked a nurse to call her mother," Gran said. "She'll be here later."

"Good," the officer said, handing me her card. "Please ring me if either of you has any information."

"Nurse, Nurse!" The old lady in the next bed called out in a tiny weak voice and my stomach tightened. I didn't like this place, I wanted Gran and me out of it, like, now.

"Well, if there's nothing more for now." WPc Williams looked at me, one eyebrow raised.

I shook my head.

"Very well." Officer Williams turned and walked away. I wanted to call her back, I felt better with her here, like, supported somehow. I didn't want to be alone with Gran in this horrible place. I didn't know what to do for her, she'd always been so strong and sure. She took care of me when I visited and now she looked so old and sad but like a little kid as well, all lost and needy.

My heart felt heavy as I turned back to Gran. Her one good eye stared at me, still silently pleading with me to make everything right, but how could I? I mean, what was I supposed to do? I couldn't undo everything that'd happened. I couldn't mend her broken arm or tell her I'd make sure nothing like this would ever happen again. I hadn't the first clue what to do. I was just so glad Mum was on her way.

"What time will Mum get here?" I asked.

"She won't."

"What?"

"I don't want your mum here."

"But, you said the nurse called her."

Gran managed a small crooked smile. "I just told the officer that so she'd leave us alone."

"Why?"

"Because your mother will fuss over me and get all upset and I don't want it. Anyway, I'm in here for now and when I go home, you'll help me."

"But what about when I go back to Rotherham?"

"Then, we'll see..."

I didn't know what she meant by that, but my stomach was spinning like the big wheel down at Luna Park. I was just a teenager and totally out of my depth. I couldn't handle this on my own.

***

I stayed with Gran until the nurses threw everybody out at the end of visiting time. By then my nails were all chewed and I felt sick.

"I'll come back tomorrow, Gran. Get better soon, okay?" I kissed her on her cheek and felt the lump come back into my throat. Walking away, I waved with every step. Gran just raised her hand. It felt like my heart was being ripped out, sticking like glue to Gran's hand. I didn't want to leave her, she didn't belong here. I wanted to pick her up and take her back to her bungalow. How could I go back there without her?

I finally turned the corner and Gran disappeared from sight. My bottom lip shook and my eyes stung, I couldn't stop them. I didn't want a whole load of people seeing me like that so I marched down between the bays and charged into the first toilets I spotted. I just managed to slam the door shut before the tears really started. I couldn't get the picture of Gran, looking so small and lost out of my mind. Grabbing some toilet paper I rolled it up and pressed it over my eyes. Like, how much time in the last five months had I spent crying in toilets? It was crazy, why were so many bad things happening?

I stood like that for ages, leaning against the door, crying like the whole world was ending. The tears just wouldn't stop.

When I finally came out of the toilet I had a banging head and my chest, nose and eyes felt like the monster of all colds. I splashed my face with water then put on makeup to cover my red nose and blotches on my neck and cheeks.

As I walked out into the empty corridor my stomach suddenly lurched again, I'd been in there, like, forever. What if they'd locked up?

There was like, nobody around. Spotting an exit sign I walked as fast as I could in that direction. I didn't run, I didn't want anybody to know I was panicking. Not that there was anybody to see me anyway. Everything was so quiet, my trainers tapping on the floor was the only sound. It was like aliens had come and beamed everybody up. After a couple of turns I spotted the exit doors and rushed forwards.

"Please let them open, please let them open."

I reached the glass doors and felt my whole body sigh with relief when they opened. I stepped outside. The air was still warm, but felt cool to my burning face. I hadn't realised just how much I'd panicked. It wasn't until later I realised how stupid I'd been. If the doors had been locked I only had to go to one of the wards and ask for help. It showed just how messed up I was. Although, it was dark now I wanted to walk, just to clear my head a bit.

I walked to Scalby Road and waited for a bus there, leaning against the nearest wall watching cars go by and trying not to think.

I couldn't face speaking to Sam so I sent her a text telling her what had happened and asking if she could stay at Gran's with me. Sam's reply came back full of concern and my eyes filled up just reading it. I blinked away more tears and when the bus arrived I thankfully climbed on, letting it take me well away from the hospital.

But later when walked onto Gran's street and her bungalow came into sight my stomach flipped over.

A heaviness settled on me as the dark windows emphasised its emptiness. With heavy feet I crossed the street then unlocked the door and walked inside, locking it behind me. Standing there, in the dark I bit my lip so hard I tasted blood. I needed a voice. Fishing out my mobile, I opened it up and speed dialed Luke.

"Hi Gorgeous. How was your second day?"

I swallowed, hard, I so wanted his arms around me right now.

"It's been awful," I croaked.

"Why, what's up?"

"It's Gran, she's been mugged, she's in hospital." My chest tightened just saying it.

"Oh, wow."

"I don't know how to handle it, Luke." Tears ran down my face again and I sniffed into the phone.

"Have you rung your mum?"

"No, Gran doesn't want me to."

"What?"

"I know, it's crazy, but she said she doesn't want Mum fussing."

"But she's got a right to know. She'd want to be there."

"I know, but I've got to do what Gran wants. Haven't I?"

The phone was silent.

"I suppose so." Luke paused, I could just about hear his brain whirring.

"Look, have you talked to Sam yet?"

"I've texted her, she's coming over."

"Good. Look, Rach, if you need me I'll come. Okay?"

"Okay."

Oh, I so wanted Luke to come, but I didn't know how long Gran would be in hospital and how much she'd need me. Somehow it would be even worse knowing Luke was in Scarborough but not having time to see him.

"Right, ring Sam, see how long she'll be, then ring me back if you want to talk some more. Okay?"

"Okay."

As soon as I ended the call, the silence in the bungalow exploded around me like an empty tomb. I shivered and quickly switched on the light, then pressed the speed dial button for Sam. Hearing her voice was like eating chocolate, so soothing.

"I'll be about half hour. Have you had anything to eat?"

"No." My stomach heaved at the thought.

"Right then, I'll order pizza and we'll have it together when I get there. Look, go get a shower and put the kettle on, that'll give you something to do. By the time you've done that I'll be there. Okay?"

Sam was fantastic. I nodded.

"Yeah, okay."

I forced my brain not to think and headed for the bathroom. Gran didn't have a shower so I settled for a soak in the tub. Sam arrived just as the pizza man climbed back in his van.

"Right, girl, lets get in there and stuff our faces, okay?" she said, pushing me back inside.

Even the smell of the pizza made me want to spew, but I nodded anyway. Sam lead the way through to the kitchen and never stopped talking. She even slept on a fold up camp bed in my bedroom and chatted until I fell asleep. I didn't have a minute to worry or feel sorry for myself all night.

I felt good the next morning when I woke up and heard the seagulls crying overhead, but it only lasted a few seconds. My stomach dropped like a coke can in a drinks machine when I remembered about Gran being in hospital.

***

"Who do you think did it?" Sam's brown eyes stared at me across the dining table in Gran's kitchen. Her chocolate hands with red and white striped finger nails were wrapped around a mug of steaming coffee.

I shrugged, "It could be anybody."

Then my mind flashed back to Joshua's parting words, 'You're gonna regret this, Brooks.'

"You don't think it could be Joshua, do you?" Sam's eyes widened.

"It could be, I mean, your gran's lived here all this time and nothing's ever happened. Then straight after you've upset Joshua, your gran gets mugged."

"Wow, thanks, Sam, for making it sound like it's all my fault."

"You know I didn't mean it like that. I'm just saying I think you might be right. But, like, what can we do about it?"

"I don't know but if it was Joshua then he's got to pay. He can't get away with it. I mean, what if he has another go at Gran?"

I could feel a burning inside me coming from my stomach all the way up into my throat. I felt like I was gonna choke. "I can't let him get away with doing this to my gran."

57

"But how can you prove it if your gran doesn't know it was him?"

"Gran knows more than she's saying, I'm sure she does. I'm gonna talk to her, try to get a description and get her to talk to the police."

"When are you going back to the hospital?"

"I'm setting off at two. Visiting starts at two thirty."

I spent the morning, cleaning Gran's bungalow, trying to make everything nice for when she came out. Sam kept grumbling that there was no point, everything in Gran's bungalow was already clean. Like, I already knew that, but I needed to keep busy.

***

Sam went home after lunch and feeling tacky after cleaning I decided on a quick bath. Just as I stepped out of it the phone rang. It split the silence so suddenly I jumped and nearly fell back into the tub.

My heart was still pounding as I picked up the receiver, a thick pink bath towel wrapped around me.

"Hello?" I asked.

'Don't let it be Gran, don't let it be Gran, let her be okay.' I chanted in my brain. I grasped the receiver so tight my fingers ached, terrified something had happened to her.

"Hello, Rachel, how is everything?"

I stopped breathing. It was Mum.

"Erm, yeah, everything's okay," I said, wanting to cross my fingers but I was too busy holding up the bath towel. I remembered shouting at Mum and Dad for lying about my adoption and now, here I was doing the same thing. But what was I supposed to do? I wanted to tell Mum the truth so she could come and

58

take charge. I didn't want to do this alone, but I had to do what Gran wanted. Didn't I?

"How's Gran?"

"Oh, er, she's fine."

"Are you having a good time?"

"Er, yeah, it's okay."

"Is there anything wrong, Rachel?"

Busted! Mum could always read me.

"Oh, er, yeah, sorry. Er, I've just got out of the bath, that's all. I'm wet through and standing here in a towel."

"Oh, I'm sorry, Love." Mum laughed. "If I know your gran, she'll be standing at your side, tutting and shaking her head at you for dripping on the carpet. I'll tell you what, you go and get dry while I have a chat with her."

My mind raced, like, what was I supposed to say?

"Oh, er, you can't, erm, yeah er, she's just got in the bath after me. GRAN! Are you in the bath yet?" I shouted. "Sorry, Mum, it's too late, she's already in."

"Oh, well, never mind." Mum sounded disappointed. "I'll talk to her later. Well, have a good time, Darling and remember we love you."

"Yeah, I know Mum. Bye."

I replaced the receiver and stood for a minute. It'd been so awkward since finding out about the adoption, it was like we were strangers or something. We used to tell each other everything but now we were like, starting all over again and lying to her was not gonna help. But what was I supposed to do?

I padded back to the bathroom and toweled myself off.

***

59

Half an hour later I caught the bus to the hospital, taxis cost *way* too much. I stared out the window the whole journey thinking about the phone call with Mum and wishing I could tell her the truth. I wanted her here with me, I didn't want to go to the hospital on my own.

Once inside I headed left towards Gran's ward, along with a stream of other visitors. I stared ahead, dreading going in, worried that Gran would be worse.

An uneasy feeling drew my eyes to a nurse in loose white tunic and blue trousers walking towards me. Her brown eyes were fixed on me, examining me. She looked sort of shocked or something, her eyes wide and mouth slightly open. She was a bit taller than me, about 5ft 5 in and really thin. Her short brown hair was spattered with grey and her face lined, like she'd had a really rough life. She just stared, her gaze never moving from my face as she came closer.

My skin prickled as we passed, it was like, totally weird. I could feel her eyes on my back as I walked on, like, what was her problem? I was really glad when I turned the corner. Still feeling a bit creepy I looked back, almost expecting her to be behind me, stalking me or something, but she wasn't. I shivered then felt like an idiot. I mean, she'd only walked past me, maybe I just looked like somebody she knew or something?

Just in case I pulled out my mirror and checked my face to make sure a huge spot hadn't erupted since I left the bungalow or something. But no, it was okay. I stuffed my mirror back into my bag, squirted some hand wash from the dispenser then walked to Gran's bay wringing my hands dry.

My stomach turned somersaults as I reached the bay, but settled a bit when I saw Gran. She must've been watching out for me and gave me this huge grin as soon as I appeared. Her eye was still swollen shut and like, purple, blue and black, but she was smiling and that made me feel loads better.

"Hi, Gran," I said, trying to sound really cheerful. "You look better."

"I feel a little better," she said, then leaned in close to me. "I'm on my best behaviour. I want to get out of here."

"Have they said anything about you going home?" Bubbles of hope fizzed up inside me like I'd just drunk a bottle of coke.

Gran shook her head, then grimaced and rubbed her neck with her hand.

"Are you okay, Gran?" The fizzy coke suddenly went flat and sunk to the bottom of my stomach.

"Oh, it's just aches and pains. As if I didn't have enough before ...." She frowned. "... you know."

"Have they given you something for it?"

"They tried to, but I'm not a tablet taker. Never have been. I don't like the things. Anyway, taking pain killers will give them an excuse to keep me longer and I'm not giving them one. I want to go home."

As we talked, I watched Gran. She did look better than yesterday, some of the fire had come back into her eyes, but there was still something missing. I just couldn't figure out what it was.

The nurses allowed me to stay right through until eight thirty when they finally kicked everybody out. We kept running out of things to say, but I just didn't want Gran to be in there all by herself for too long. Gran managed to get out of bed and we wandered up and down the wards for a bit. She was really careful because the floors were so smooth and her slippers did exactly that, they kept slipping. In the end I linked

61

arms with her and we walked real slow, so Gran was okay.

By the time I went home I felt a bit better about her. I told myself she was doing real well to say it was only one day since she was mugged. It was still hard waving goodbye though. I just *so* wanted to take her back to the bungalow with me.

Once outside, I walked across the car park, heading for Scalby Road. Just as I passed the mini roundabout with a huge hospital sign on it, I felt shivers in my spine again. Looking over my shoulder, I saw her, the same nurse, standing just outside the hospital doors, staring at me again. My blood dropped ten degrees, I mean, what was her problem? Was she some psycho or what?

'Don't be stupid, Rachel!' I forced myself to turn away from her and keep walking. *'She's probably just on her break and nipped out for a ciggy or something. I mean, why would she be staring at me? She doesn't know me. It's just a coincidence.'*

I still couldn't stop the shiver slipping down my back. I could feel her eyes drilling into me all along the hospital road until it finally turned enough and I was hidden behind the renal unit.

When I reached the main road I risked a quick look back. The road behind me was empty except for an old couple chatting as they walked. My shoulders sagged with relief, I'd been scared she'd follow me or something.

'You see,' I told myself, *'You're just being a paranoid idiot, she wasn't watching you at all.'*

It's weird though, because I really didn't believe myself.

CHAPTER SIX

"How's your gran?"

Sam was leaning against the bungalow door when I got back.

"Have you been here long?"

"Nah, I've been with the girls checking out some lads on the beach. Talk about six packs! You should've seem 'em." Sam must have seen the envious look on my face. "Sorry. I know you wish your gran was okay and you could be out with us."

"Not much of a holiday is it?" I said, unlocking the door.

"Have they said anything about your gran coming home yet?"

"No." I locked the door and dropped my bag on a chair in the sitting room. I didn't really know what else to say. "Fancy a drink?"

"Yeah, I'll have a hot chocolate. You got any chocolate?" Sam raised her eyebrows.

"Yeah, Gran always has some drinking chocolate in."

Sam tutted and shook her head.

"No, you wally. I mean some real chocolate. I think we should just veg and pig out. We'll order a take away, put a film on, melt some chocolate on a plate and have drinking chocolate with it."

I smiled. "That sounds perfect."

Forty minutes later we were both laying on our stomachs on Gran's soft hearth rug surrounded by empty chinese take away cartons. A plate of melted chocolate sat between us and '17 Again' played on the television.

"Zac Effron is such a hotty," Sam said, with a sigh.

"Hmn. I prefer Chad Michael Murray," I said, licking a chocolate coated finger.

"A Cinderella Story? You would," said Sam. "A Luke look alike."

I just grinned a self satisfied grin. I still couldn't believe I was going out with somebody as hot as Luke Chambers.

By the time I climbed into bed, I was rested, happy and feeling just a little bit sick. Sam slipped down onto the camp bed again in my room. Even though Gran wasn't there it just didn't feel right for Sam to use her bed.

"Night," I said, snuggling under the covers.

"Don't let the bedbugs bite." Sam's muffled reply came from deep in her pillow.

**

My stomach flipped over when I woke up the next morning. The last thing I wanted was to go back to the hospital again. I wished Gran was well and home again.

"Do you want me to come with you?" Sam asked over a bowl full of Cornflakes.

Did I ever.

"Will you? I run out of things to talk about after a bit and there's this creepy nurse ..." As soon as I'd said it, I wished I hadn't.

"A what? A creepy nurse?" Sam was suddenly sitting to attention on the kitchen chair opposite me, her eyes sparkling. "Tell all!"

64

"Well. It's just that she's like, you know, always around and like, staring at me or something. It's weird. I mean, she's hasn't done anything, she just sort of, stares."

"Maybe she fancies you."

"Yeow! Don't say that! That'd be too gross!"

"Not for some people."

"Well it would be for me, okay. Anyway, she's old."

"What, like sixty or something?"

"No, more like forty, I think."

"That is old. So, what time are you going…?"

The phone rang before Sam finished and my stomach turned to mush. What if it was about Gran, bad news or something?

"Hello?" My throat was already closing up and my voice came out all shaky.

"Hello, Rachel?"

"Gran!" I couldn't believe it. Gran's voice was the last one I expected to hear. My stomach settled, she was all right, she was on the phone. Then it flopped again, what if she was ringing with bad news, like she needed an operation or something?

"Yes, it's me, Love. They say I can come home today ..."

My heart jumped in my chest and did a 360 degree somersault.

"Can you bring me some clean clothes and arrange a taxi?"

My face nearly cracked, my smile was so wide.

"Yeah, sure, Gran. Can I come now or do I have to wait until visiting time?"

"They say I can go as soon as I'm ready."

"Right. I'll be there in about an hour, I'll get everything together and come straight away. See you

65

soon! Love you!" I hung up and bounced into the kitchen to Sam.

"Gran's coming home! I've got to take her some clothes and go get her now!"

Sam's wide grin covered her face, her fantastically white teeth gleaming.

"Do you still want me to come?"

"Yeah, please, you can carry the bags while I help Gran."

"Oh, great, I can come and be the bell boy, er, girl. Whatever."

Sam finished her breakfast but I couldn't finish mine. I just wanted Gran out of that place as soon as possible before they could change their minds.

***

An hour later we walked into Gran's bay and I froze. My mouth flopped open like a hungry fish and I just stared. Gran was in her side chair with the freaky nurse sitting on her bed talking to her.

The nurse looked up at me, all smiles, her brown eyes fixed on mine like they were drilling into me, examining my soul or something. I wanted to ask her what she wanted and why she was talking to Gran but no sound came out.

The nurse turned her bright smile back to Gran.

"Well, I see your granddaughter has come to take you home, so I'll be on my way. I hope all goes well for you. Take care."

"I will. Thank you." Gran reached up and shook her hand. The nurse put her other hand on Gran's, like a hand hug, then headed towards me, her eyes scanning my face. She nodded as she passed.

I didn't move until she was out of the bay, then I rushed forward and flopped down on the bed. It was warm underneath me and I quickly shuffled onto a cold spot.

"What did *she* want?"

"Oh, she's really nice. She wanted to know whether I'll be all right. She was very happy when I told her you were staying with me for a while and would look after me. She wanted to know all about you."

My hands tightened on the edge of the bed, squeezing the sheets between my fingers. My brain tripped over itself running through loads of scary scenarios. I felt hunted, like in one of those films, you know, where a weirdo, follows you, takes over your life then kills you or dies trying.

I looked up at Sam, telling her with my eyes that it was her, but Sam just stared blankly back at me. I gave up and decided to just get Gran out of there as soon as I could and hopefully never see the nurse again.

"Are you ready then, Gran?"

"Yes, Love, they brought my tablets ten minutes ago. It was that nice nurse who brought them, I forget her name."

I shivered at the mention of her and quickly called for a taxi.

"Okay, then, Gran, let's go." I looped my arm into hers and Sam grabbed the little overnight bag. "Are you sure you've got everything?"

"Yes, Love, the nice nurse checked for me."

"Good," I said, wrinkling my nose. I wasn't happy about anything that nurse did. I didn't trust her, not one micro metre. I lead Gran outside and didn't relax until the taxi had taken us clear of the hospital. Gran was finally on her way home. Hopefully now she could mend and get back to normal and I'd never see that weird nurse again.

CHAPTER SEVEN

"Do you want to come to the beach, Gran?"

Gran had been home a week now. She was walking fine and the bruises had faded, but she still hadn't been out of the bungalow. It was like, she'd suddenly become a hermit or something.

"No, I'm all right here, Love. I have some ironing to do."

"But it's roasting, Gran. Can't you do the ironing later when it cools off? You need some fresh air."

"I have plenty of fresh air here. I have all the windows open and all I need." Gran widened her arm to take in the kitchen. Every surface sparkled and there wasn't a single pot in the sink. From her first day home she'd gone cleaning crazy, even with one wrist still in pot. The whole place shone like an operating theatre. If I left so much as a finger print on a mirror Gran appeared behind me, tutting and rubbing until all evidence of my presence had gone. She was like, manic. I know she's always been clean but this was ridiculous! I felt like a virus that had to be wiped out!

I'd tried to talk to her about the attack but each time she put me off.

"Oh, Rachel, I don't want to think about it now." Or.

"I'm too tired and anyway, what does it matter now? It's over."

Earlier, at breakfast, I'd tried for about the fifth time to get her to describe the attacker.

"Gran, have you remembered anything about the person who mugged you?" I asked, scooping up a spoonful of cornflakes and trying to look casual.

"Rachel, don't start, I've had enough questions from the police." Gran put down her toast and picked up her mug.

"Yes, but Gran, they asked us to contact them if you remembered any more."

"Well, I haven't, so I won't be contacting them, will I?" Gran said, sipping her steaming tea.

"Can't you remember anything? His hair colour, size, what he was wearing?"

Gran slammed her mug down onto the kitchen table, making tea slop over onto the wooden surface.

"Look, just leave it will you?" She snapped, fixing me with her fiercest glare, "I've told you I don't remember, if I had anything to say I would talk to the police, not you. Now leave it alone! In fact, go on out and see your friends, I'm tired of you hanging around here!"

I felt my eyes sting. She couldn't have hurt me more if she'd physically slapped me. I bit my lip and stirred my cornflakes, keeping my eyes down. I'd never seen her so angry before.

"Oh, Rachel, I'm sorry, Love," Gran said, more softly. "It's just that I've told you all I can. There's nothing more for me to say. I just wish you'd stop bothering me about it. Leave it alone. Let me put it behind me."

Even her words told me there was more, 'I've told you all I can', not 'I've told you everything'. But what could I do? I just hoped she'd open up eventually. Before then I'd have to figure out a way to help her myself.

70

"I've got to do something about Gran," I said later, stretched out on a beach towel.

"Why, what's up?" Summer rolled over and passed me her sun cream. "Here, rub some of that on my back."

I sat up and squeezed the slimy cream onto my hand and smeared it over Summer's back.

"She won't go out. Since she came out of hospital the furthest she's been is to the wheelie bin and back. I can't get her to go anywhere."

"Do you think she's scared?" Ruby rubbed her nose and looked across at me.

"Doh! 'Course she's scared. But, like, what can I do about it?"

Everybody lay silent, until Sam yelled as two ten-year-old boys ran past.

"Hey! Watch out!" She sat up, spitting into the sand. "Those idiots just jumped right over my head and showered me with sand! Pugh! I got a right gob full!"

"You shouldn't have been laying there with your mouth open," said Ruby, grinning.

"For your information, 'Miss Know-it-All', I was just about to say something, that's why my mouth was open. I was gonna say, give her time. She's only been out of hospital a week, she's probably still nervous. She'll get over it in time."

"Trouble is, she hasn't got time. I'm going home in a couple of weeks and she's got to be able to get out and do her shopping and everything. I mean, what's gonna happen to her if she's still too scared to go out by the time I go home?"

"Has she actually said she's scared?" Ruby hitched up her white bikini top and turned onto her back. "I mean, can't you talk to her, reason with her, you know?"

"No, she's not actually said it. She just keeps making up excuses about why she can't come out. Today it's ironing. Yesterday it was cleaning! I mean, have you seen Gran's bungalow recently? Anybody'd think nobody lived there it's so clean. Dust daren't come anywhere near it and spiders are boycotting the place. One hint of a speck of dust or a web and the fluffy mop's out. A spider's got no chance."

"What you need then, is to find out who mugged her, get some evidence and get them locked up. If your Gran knows they're behind bars, then I reckon she'll start going out again." Sam leaned on one arm and looked across at me. "Don't you think?"

"I can't get her to tell me anything about the attacker but it's got to be Joshua. I mean, this happened just after he threatened me. It's got to be him. But, like, there's no way he's gonna confess and I haven't a clue how to prove it." I looked across Ruby and Summer who were laid sizzling in the sun like rashers of bacon. Summer wore the tiniest pink bikini you've ever seen, it barely covered her 'bits'. Ruby was bigger, her stomach escaping over the top of her bikini bottoms.

Sam sat facing me, her black bikini and perfect figure had every man and boy drooling as they went past.

"Then we've got to find a way to make him confess," she said.

"Oh yeah, like he's just gonna head into the police station and say 'please officer it was me, will you lock me up?'" I said, "Get real. He's never gonna do that."

Just then Sapphire come back, juggling five ice creams in her small hands.

"Grab 'em quick or you'll be wearing 'em. I'm gonna drop 'em!"

Two were tilting so far towards me, the flakes were hanging out. I reached up and grabbed them quick, then yelped as a blob of freezing chocolate ice cream landed on my ankle.

"Yewh!" I cried, passing one of the cones to Ruby before it had chance to drop any more dollops on me.

Sam took two cones off Sapphire while I licked round the bottom of mine and straightened up my flake.

"Sorry about dropping the ice cream on you," Sapphire said, plonking down on the towel next to my feet.

"It's all right," I said, wiping my ankle with a tissue.

Sapphire smiled, her cheeks pink then turned her attention to her own cone.

"So, what are we gonna do about Gran?" I said.

"What if we all come round and go to the shops or somethin'. She'd have to feel safe with all of us there, wouldn't she?" said Summer, squinting up at me.

I shrugged. "Maybe."

"Hey Summer, are you gonna sit up and take this ice cream off me or am I just gonna have to eat it?" Sam asked, a chocolate cone in one hand and a strawberry one in the other.

Summer sat up quickly and grabbed the pink cone as my bag vibrated against my leg and JLS sang out. Fishing inside, I pulled out my mobile and grinned when I saw Luke's name.

"Hey, Baby!"

Sam grinned. I ignored her.

"Hi. Guess what?" Luke's voice sent warm tingles down my spine as I pictured his muscles straining against a white T-shirt.

"No, what?"

"You'll never guess."

"What, Luke? What's up?" I pulled my legs up under my chin then slid them down again. I didn't know whether to be excited or nervous.

"Aran's only gone and got chicken pox!"

"Chicken pox! When?"

"Who's got chicken pox, Luke?" Sam leaned forward, trying to hear, but I just shook my head and didn't answer.

"Found out this morning. He says he was like, real spotty yesterday and his mum took him to the doc today. Anyway, he says the holiday's off, he can't go. So his family's cancelled it."

"Oh, Luke, I'm sorry. You were really looking forward to that."

"Yeah, well. It would've been a laugh going camping with his family. Anyway, I thought, seeing as I can't go there, maybe I could come to you, now your Gran's home."

"Come here?" My heart jumped up, flipped over and kept spinning.

"Yeah. I mean, I'd stay in a guest house like, but we could see each other."

"That'd be great. When can you come?"

"I'll check out buses and trains and stuff for tomorrow. Mum says it's okay, so long as I check in with her every day. But is it okay with you? How's your gran doing?"

"Just the same, she won't go out. I'm staying in with her as much as I can but it's driving me nuts. I'm worried sick. We've just been talking about what we can do to get her outside."

"Come up with anything?"

"Not really. Except that we need to get Joshua to confess."

"Wish you luck with that one! Well, we'll see what we can come up with tomorrow. Okay?"

"Yeah, see you then. Text me later and let me know when you're coming and I'll meet you."

"Will do."

I snapped my phone shut with a grin so wide it almost stretched off the end of my face.

"Luke's coming tomorrow. So, when he gets here, we'll get together and figure out how to make Joshua confess. Okay?"

Everybody nodded but I could see they weren't convinced. I was gonna have to do some serious thinking.

***

The next day I stood waiting for Luke's bus with the sun frying my skin. I'd put sun lotion on but felt like that was just the fat I was frying in. I'd got my shortest blue shorts and tiniest white top on and with most of my body uncovered I was melting. I'd fastened my hair up with a band and grips but even that hadn't helped much. I backed away from the road to shelter under a tree at the edge of West Square. It wasn't much cooler under there but at least I wasn't an easy target for the sun.

I smiled with relief when a familiar looking coach pulled in. Standing on tiptoe, I strained to see Luke and suddenly there he was halfway down the bus, queuing to get off. His hand brushed his beautiful blond hair out of his eyes and my heart twirled. I couldn't keep still and bounced up and down like a three-year-old.

"Luke!" I shouted, waving like crazy. "Luke!"

He turned to the window and his face broke into this fantastic grin. My whole body turned to instant mush. I had to drop down off my toes because my legs had gone all wobbly. We'd been going out for three months, but he could still turn me into Playdo. Rushing to the door, I flung myself into his arms the second his feet hit the ground. I reckon I surprised him as he staggered backwards and nearly ended up on top of an old woman behind him. He grabbed the edge of the door and managed to stop himself before we both hit the deck. Luke straightened up, his face feeling flushed and warm next to mine and wrapped his arms around me.

"I reckon you've missed me," he said, grinning.

It might have been just over a week since I last saw him but it felt more like a month. His body was so strong and firm against mine. Our lips locked and I was lost, somewhere in the Caribbean I think. I could've just stayed there forever but I had to come up for air and the old lady was still stuck on the bus behind Luke. She shook her head and muttered something about 'young people these days'.

"Oh, Luke," I said at last. "I've really missed you and I've been doing my head in worrying about Gran."

"Oh, and I suppose you haven't missed me at all?" Rebecca's voice, laced with her usual sarcasm and sounding just like mine, came from behind the old lady. "When you've finished sucking his face the rest of us would like to get off this roasting bus. I'm cooking in here."

"Rebecca? I didn't know you were coming."
We stepped aside and I grinned as her head appeared
when the tutting old woman stepped down. Rebecca
followed her. She was wearing a light blue T-shirt and
blue shorts just like mine. Her short brown hair was
wet because of the heat and stuck to her forehead. Her
tanned face, identical to mine, grinned back at me.

She shrugged. "Figured you might need some
brains on the subject. Anyway it's about time I met my
step adoptive gran."

Luke frowned at her. "Your what?"

Rebecca shrugged again. "Well, like, what else
am I supposed to call her? She's my sister's adoptive
gran. Whatever, it's still time I met her. So, are you
gonna help us with our bags, or what?"

"Yeah, sure." I turned towards the back of the
bus and that's when I saw him. Joshua Green sitting on
the low wall of the train station opposite, his face set
like a bull terrier, glaring at Luke. I froze, my heart
pounding. Why did Joshua have to be around here
again? Like, weren't there better places to hang out? I
mean, watching buses and trains unload isn't exactly
the thrill of the week, is it? But then I had a scary
thought, he'd been at the park when I was there as well.
Was he following me? Okay, he could've been waiting
for a bus home, he was kind of near the bus stops but it
was a bit too much of a coincidence for me.

"Let's get your bags quick and go." I pulled
Luke towards the back of the bus.

"What's up?" Luke frowned down at me.

"Joshua Green's, over there." I nodded in his
direction, still tugging at Luke.

"The one you think mugged your gran?" he
asked, twisting around to see.

"Yeah."

"Looks a right head case," Rebecca muttered. "Let's go and have it out with him now."

She stepped towards the road, but I grabbed her arm.

"No! Not now, we've got to think about it first. Don't make it worse. Come on, let's just get out of here!"

Rebecca turned back and grabbed her bag but I could see her narrowed eyes flitting over to Joshua.

I finally managed to pull them both away, but my heart didn't slow down until we'd grabbed a taxi and Joshua was well out of sight.

"We should've had it out with him." Rebecca frowned at me.

"But what am I supposed to say? I mean, I'm pretty sure it's him after what he said. Has Luke told you about it?"

"Yes." Rebecca nodded.

"So, I reckon it's him but I've got no proof."

"I don't think you can do anything yet, I mean, you can't just go around making accusations. There's a load of people out there who'd mug someone, you know, druggies and that." Luke looked down at me and I knew he was right. I snuggled closer to him in the back seat, holding his arm and feeling the muscles tense beneath his T-shirt. I ran my fingers through the hairs on his lower arm and gazed up, melting.

"Ugh, if you're going to get all gooey I'm out of here. I'll walk the rest of the way."

I pulled my gaze away from Luke and stuck my tongue out at Rebecca.

"Hey, turn around if you don't want to see," I said.

"You're embarrassing the driver," Rebecca said, trying to look serious in the front passenger seat.

"Yeah, sure. I bet he's seen it all," Luke muttered.

"You can bet I have," the taxi driver winked at us through the rear view mirror. "And then some!"

We pulled up outside Luke's B & B, paid the driver and climbed out.

"Okay, we'll get Luke booked in and drop his bags off, then take yours to Gran's bungalow, I'm sure she'll let you stay," I said, "Gran'll be real happy to see you, she's been asking about you both since I got here. Well, until she went into hospital that is. She hasn't said much about anything since she got out."

My stomach tightened, just thinking about the change in Gran depressed me.

"Well, with a few people around she might feel safer then maybe she'll tell us what happened." Rebecca said.

I hoped so.

CHAPTER EIGHT

"Wait outside, I'll go in first."

Leaving Luke and Rebecca on the doorstep, I unlocked Gran's door and walked into the quiet bungalow.

"Gran? Are you there, Gran?"

"And where else would I be?" Gran's head appeared around the kitchen door. "Come on in here and help me clear up. I've been baking all afternoon and that is not an easy task with one arm in a pot. Especially with this plastic bag wrapped around it." She held up her plastic coated pot as evidence. "I could have done with you an hour ago when I ran out of butter. I had to get some from old Mrs Mathers next door."

"You went round there?" I followed Gran into the kitchen, my eyes wide, this was a major step forward.

"No, of course not. I was up to my arms in pastry. I rang her and she brought it round."

My shoulders slumped. I didn't like to point out that to use the phone Gran must have washed her hands, in which case there was nothing to stop her going next door.

"Gran, there's a couple of people wanting to see you."

Gran's eyes flicked, a look of panic flashing across her face.

"Can't you see I'm too busy, young Rachel? I have no time to be going visiting right now."

"No, Gran. You don't have to go any where, they've come here to see you."

"Here?" Gran's hands tightened around the pastry in the bowl, making it squeeze out of each side of her fists. "Who is it?"

I chewed my lip, maybe this wasn't such a good idea after all. What if it made Gran worse?

"It's er, it's Luke and Rebecca."

Gran blinked, colour coming back into her fingers as she released the pastry. "Your young man and your new sister?"

I nodded.

"Well, well. They're here?" Gran craned her neck to see around me. "Where?"

"They're out front."

"You left them outside? Where are your manners, Rachel Brooks? Go on, go get them whilst I wash my hands."

Pastry flicked off Gran's fingers and hit me on the chest as she shooed me away. I squirmed as a piece slipped down my cleavage.

"Okay, Gran," I said, turning and fishing down inside my top trying to retrieve the cold chunk of pastry. I pulled it out then couldn't figure out what to do with it. In the end I took it to the door and flung it outside when I let Luke and Rebecca in. Luke gave me this, 'What are you doing, you crazy chick?' kind of a look, but I couldn't be bothered explaining, I just waved them inside.

As I closed the door something in the corner of my eye stopped me. I opened the door wider and looked out properly. Ice shot through my heart. Over by the end of the street, almost hidden by a lamp post stood a woman, with short brown hair. She only wore a thin blouse now, but even without the smock I recognised her. It was the creepy nurse from the hospital.

I shoved the door shut quickly, a shiver shooting through me. I guess I'd gone pale because Rebecca gave me this look when I turned around.

"What's up?"

I shook my head.

"Nothing."

Now wasn't the time. I didn't want Gran overhearing anything.

"Rachel?" Luke frowned down at me. "There is summat wrong. What is it?"

Shaking my head again, I whispered, "Tell you later," and lead them through to the kitchen.

"Hey, Gran, this is Luke and Rebecca."

Gran had removed the plastic bag and washed her hands. She slipped the towel back on its hook and walked right up to Rebecca, her head on one side like an enquiring puppy.

"Now let me have a good look at you." She shook her head. "Amazing. I'm sorry to stare but you are so like my Rachel. You are just as pretty too."

"Gran!" I felt my cheeks burning. Rebecca just grinned.

"Never you mind!" Gran wagged her finger at me. "No matter what you say, you are a pretty girl and young Rebecca here is your double, so she is just as pretty too. And you ..." She moved over to Luke, "I can see what Rachel sees in you. A handsome face and good physique. Why, if I was younger, I would fancy you myself."

"Gran!" I hissed. Luke's face went from pale pink to bright red in just two seconds. He was like, shuffling his feet, trying to smile and looking anywhere but at Gran.

"You're not embarrassed are you?" Gran sounded sorry, but I could see the mischievous twinkle in her eyes and her tongue in her check and my heart lifted. Finally a little bit of my old Gran was back. "Now where are my manners? Come, sit you all down and we'll have a nice cup of tea."

I knew for a fact that Rebecca hates tea, but for once she didn't say exactly what she thought, instead she smiled and said, "Thank you very much, Mrs Banks"

***

Later, when we went outside to walk Luke back to his B & B I was almost bouncing.

"I can't believe how much better she is, it's like, you've brought her back to life or something. She was like, really playing up to you both, tormenting you and everything!" I grabbed both their hands. "Thanks for coming. I mean it." I could feel my eyes stinging, tears prickling my eyelashes. "I've been so worried about her, I thought the old Gran was gone for good, now I think that maybe she'll be all right again."

Luke swallowed and Rebecca did as well, they blinked a lot too. I reckon they were feeling as emotional as me.

"Well, I hope she'll be okay. I'll come back round again tomorrow, all right?" Luke said.

I nodded.

"Look, why don't you walk Luke back to the B & B so you can be on your own a bit. I'll wait for you here," Rebecca suggested.

"Are you sure?" I asked, hopefully. I'd only been away a few days but I'd missed him like crazy.

Rebecca grimaced. "Like you'd miss me."

She turned and went back into the bungalow. As we went through the gate I let my hand brush against Luke's and a thrill surged through me when he held it.

We talked all the way to Queen's Parade, about everything and anything. I felt light and free, better than I'd felt for days.

While we waited for a taxi to take me back to Gran's we crossed the road and stood looking down over Royal Albert Drive. Way below the sea crashed against the grey sea wall, sending showers of white foam up onto the road.

"I'm glad you're here, Luke." I looked up into his deep blue eyes.

He put his arms around me and drew me in, pressing me against his chest. I could feel him breathing, his chest rising and falling. He leaned down and we kissed. It was so romantic with the sounds of the waves below and seagulls calling above us. I could have stayed that way all evening but the blast of a car horn right next to us nearly gave me a heart attack.

"You call a taxi, Love?" The driver asked, leaning across his passenger seat.

I nodded. It seemed so early to be leaving Luke on his first day, but I wanted to get back to Gran. She'd only just met Rebecca and might feel awkward being alone with her too long.

Luke turned to go and reluctantly I released him. I watched him walk to his B & B and give me a last wave, the wind blowing his blond hair across his eyes. I've got the hottest boyfriend ever!

I opened the back door of the taxi and slipped one leg in. Just before I slid in completely I heard a shout.

"Rachel!"

I looked down the road and stopped breathing. Hurrying towards me on the other side of the road was the nurse.

"No!" I gasped.

"You all right?" The taxi driver turned in his seat.

"Er, yeah," I said and climbed in feeling her eyes drilling into the back of my head, making my skin crawl.

"Rachel!"

I twisted in my seat. She'd got her arm raised and was running towards me now.

"Can we go please?" I begged, "Quickly."

The taxi pulled out and I watched her fade into the distance, frantically waving at me. I faced forwards, relieved when we turned the corner, but I couldn't settle. My hands shook in my lap. She'd followed us to Luke's B & B. Now she knew where to find Luke and Gran. This was getting way too serious. She was really creeping me out now.

CHAPTER NINE

"What's up with you?"

Rebecca leaned against the kitchen door frame, as I slammed the front door and rushed down the hall. I grabbed her shoulders and bungled her into the kitchen.

"Where's Gran?" I hissed.

"In her room, getting ready for bed. Why?"

"It's that nurse, she's stalking me."

Rebecca snorted. "Yeah, right, like she's got nothing better to do."

"No seriously." I grasped her arm. "I mean it. She was outside earlier when you and Luke came in and then outside Luke's B & B just now. She must have followed us. She waved at me and shouted my name."

"So what did she want?"

"I don't know, I just got out of there, fast."

Rebecca grinned. "You're winding me up, aren't you?"

"No. Seriously." I eyed Rebecca. "You do believe me, don't you?"

Rebecca shrugged. "Yeah, I suppose. What did Luke say?"

"He didn't see her, he'd just gone in."

Rebecca shrugged again, "Look, next time you see her tell me and I'll go sort her out."

"You won't."

"I will."

"No way. She could be, like, psycho. She's fixated on me or something and you look like me. She might go for you with an axe or something."

"Did you see an axe?" Rebecca grinned.

"No. But I'm telling you. Stay away from her."

"I'll get you a coke." Rebecca turned to the fridge.

"Rebecca?"

"Look, I'm making no promises. But I'll not take any chances, okay?" She reached into the fridge and pulled out a coke.

I took the cold can from her.

"Look, just be careful, okay?"

"Okay."

I wasn't entirely happy with that but there was nothing more I could do.

All night I dreamt I was being chased by a crazed axe-wielding nurse up and down the halls of Scarborough hospital. She eventually cornered me in pathology and taunted me about a bare slab waiting for me. I raced around rattling every door, desperately trying to get out, but all were locked, even the one I'd just come through. I cowered in a corner with no where left to run while she laughed psychotically. Suddenly Gran was beside me, calling, 'Rachel, Rachel. Save me!' a look of terror on her face. I stood in front of her to keep her safe but then she started to push me from behind. I tried to resist but she was pushing me straight into the path of the swinging axe...

I woke with a jump. Gran was shaking me.

"Rachel, wake up, it's morning."

My heart was pounding so hard I thought it'd burst and I was soaked in sweat.

"Come on, sleepy head. I've been trying to wake you for five minutes. Dead to the world you were."

"Sorry, Gran." I pushed myself up and slid my legs over the side of the bed as Gran left the room. Yawning, I stood up. My legs felt wobbly and weak.

"I must've run a flipping marathon last night," I muttered, walking carefully out to the bathroom.

I reached for the door handle then jumped as it suddenly swung open and Rebecca bounced out shouting, "Hi, Rach!"

"Don't *do* that!" I gasped, holding my heart.

"Sorry," said Rebecca, grinning. "Rough night?"

"How'd you know?"

"Oh, because you shouted 'go away, leave me alone' all night and thrashed about so much I thought you were going to run right out of the bed and land on me. And then there's your face. Have you looked in the mirror yet? You'd look good in 'Night of the living dead' or summat."

I rolled my eyes with my last bit of energy.

"Very funny. I'm gonna have a shower. Make me some breakfast will you?"

"What did your last slave die of?" Rebecca headed for the kitchen but looked back over her shoulder. "Oh, by the way, your Gran's dusting the sitting room."

"But she dusted that yesterday!" I shook my head. "We've seriously got to get her out of the house today."

Rebecca shrugged. "We can try."

***

Two hours later Luke knocked at the door and we'd still not persuaded Gran to come with us. She'd just come up with loads of excuses.

"My hair is a mess, it needs a perm."

"Well, we'll take you to the hair dresser's then."

"No, my neck's sore, it will just have to wait until I feel better."

"What if we get a hairdresser to come here, then you can go out with us later?"

"Too expensive."

"I could perm it for you." That was Rebecca.

"Not likely!"

"I'm good at it, I've done my mum's."

"I only have your word for that. No, I'll wait until I'm well enough to go the hairdressers."

We tried all sorts but didn't get anywhere. We both knew the real reason though, she was scared. Her hair looked fine and it'd never kept her in before. I mean, okay, her wrist was still broken but that wouldn't stop her going out. All her other bruises had faded and she looked fine. Anyway, the way she was cleaning the bungalow like a mad woman, she couldn't be feeling that bad.

"Are you sure you won't come, Gran?" I asked one last time.

"Oh, stop bothering me, Rachel. I've told you 'no'. Now get on all of you, I have work to do." She wafted us away like annoying flies and I finally gave up.

I walked outside, my shoulders and head slumped.

"I thought she was getting better, she was so lively when you both came yesterday. I thought she was gonna be okay."

"You'll have to give her time." Luke's voice was way too calm.

"I can't, Luke! Don't you get it? I haven't got time. I've got to go home in two weeks. What's gonna happen to her if she isn't sorted by then?"

"You'll have to tell your mum," said Rebecca.

"I can't, I promised. And anyway, what's Mum gonna do? She'll be with me in Rotherham and Gran'll

89

be here on her own.   It's no good, we've got to do something about Joshua. If I could just tell her, he's locked up, then maybe she'll come out again."

"And how are you going to pull that one off?" Rebecca said, her voice ringing with sarcasm as we walked towards town. "Go up to him and say, 'Hey Joshua, how about turning yourself in?'"

"You're not helping," said Luke. He slipped his strong, warm arm around my waist and I breathed in the mixture of soap and recently sun-tanned skin. Even with all that was going on, it felt good walking beside him again.

His arm must have woken something in me because a light bulb suddenly pinged on in my head.

"Rebecca might be right."

"What?" Both Luke and Rebecca stared at me, open-mouthed.

"Well, it can't hurt, can it? We go up to him, tell him we know he did it and he'd better turn himself in or we'll go to the police."

"We can't go to the police, we've got no proof," said Luke.

"Yes, but Joshua doesn't know that, does he? We could pretend we have witnesses and it'd be in his own best interests to turn himself in first."

Luke shook his head. "He'll never buy that."

"He might," said Rebecca, her forehead creased into a little frown. "I mean, we've got nothing to lose."

"Except our necks," muttered Luke.

***

"I can't believe we're actually doing this," I said, as we walked towards West Square, one of Joshua's favourite hang outs.

90

"Well, it was your idea," said Rebecca.

"Actually it was yours," said Luke.

"Whatever." Rebecca shrugged.

"He's not here." I looked around the square but there was no sign of him leaning against the trees or across at the train station. "Where else does he hang out these days?"

"How should I know?" said Rebecca. "You're the one who comes from around here. Ask your friend Sam."

"Can't, she's out with her family today and her dad makes her turn off her mobile, he hates the things. A real technophobe. I'll try Ruby and Summer, they're out shopping with Ruby's mum." I pulled out my mobile and sent a text.

'Do u no where josh green hangs? Rach'

We crossed the road and sat on the low wall outside the train station, watching a constant tide of passengers stepping on and off buses. It was ten minutes before my phone beeped.

"Is that all you've got, a beep?" asked Rebecca.

I shrugged. "Works for me. It plays a tune when it rings. It'll do."

Rebecca rolled her eyes.

'He hangs @ castle bone yard. Ru'

I groaned. A cemetery, trust Joshua. The phone beeped again.

'Check top Peasholm in trees. Sum'

"Wonder what he gets up to there?" said Luke.

"Don't ask," I muttered. "Well, I reckon we should try the cemetery first."

"Why?" asked Rebecca.

"Because Peasholm's down hill and if we're wrong we'll have to come all the way back up again," I said. "And it's a hot day, so there'll be like, tons of holiday makers in there. No, I reckon he'll be at the cemetery, it's quieter."

"You know we could walk around all day and never find him?" Rebecca grumbled.

"Well it was your idea," I said, arms folded.

"It wasn't a serious one. I *was* being sarcastic at the time," Rebecca frowned back.

"Yeah, well. I've got to try something and unless you can think of anything better ...?"

Rebecca shrugged. "Whatever. But if we're going to do all that walking, I need supplies." She nodded towards the train station. "Are there any vending machines in there?"

Five minutes later and not a bit of change left between us, we left the station each clutching a can of coke, a bag of crisps and a couple of chocolate bars.

"Real healthy," I muttered.

"Don't worry about it, we'll have walked it off before we've done today," said Rebecca, taking a bite out of her mars bar.

I took them the shortest route, but we were still boiling by the time we got to St. Mary's Church.

"The radio at the B & B said it was going to rain today," Luke said, running the back of his hand across his soaking forehead.

"They always get Scarborough weather wrong. Ask anybody who lives here," I answered. "There he is." I pointed.

We stood in the grounds of the church over looking a grassed area with bent old trees casting cool shadows. Old gravestones removed from their places zigzagged back to back across the grass like a fossilized snake. I pointed over to the furthest corner. Joshua sat in the shadow of a huge tree with his back against the dark outer wall, almost hidden by the redundant gravestones. He was alone.

We walked behind the stones and headed towards him. Joshua watched us all the way, his legs stretched out in front and crossed at the ankles. A smile played on his lips and a cigarette hung from his mouth.

"So, this is the boyfriend then?" he said, sneering at Luke like he was a cheap imitation watch or something. "You should've stuck with me chick."

"We need to talk Joshua," I said, ignoring him.

Joshua pulled in his legs and stood, leaning against the wall.

"What? You been telling your boyfriend what we've been up to? Is he jealous or somethin'?"

I shrivelled inside. I hadn't told Luke about Joshua touching me up.

"We haven't been up to anything and you know it!" I snapped, glancing across at Luke. He managed not to show anything, but I knew I was gonna have some explaining to do later.

"Anything you say babe." Joshua sneered at Luke, "She's hot that girl friend of yours, hope you're man enough to handle her. Hey, maybe your sister here wants some of the action. I've heard about you but now I see you..." He leered at Rebecca, his eyes raking over her just like he'd done to me. "I mean, you're her double, yeah? Just as hot but maybe a bit more willing? What about it, eh? You up for some fun, or what?"

Rebecca's hands slammed onto her hips.

"I wouldn't let a snake like you touch me if everybody else turned into vampires and you were the only human left," she spat.

Joshua grinned. "Ooh, a fiesty one. I like that. Just watch where you're walking, you never know where I might be lurking."

93

"You'll leave them both alone!" Luke stepped forward, his body rigid and fists clenched. I reckon he'd figured out what'd happened with me and Joshua.

I put my hand on his arm.

"Look Joshua, we know what you did to Gran, we've got witnesses. You'd better turn yourself in, or we will."

One corner of Joshua's mouth turned up into a sneer. "Or else what? You don't have any witnesses cos I never touched your gran. Old bags aren't my thing. Enjoyed hearing about it though."

A wave of doubt washed over me, what if I was wrong?

Joshua carried on. "If she's your gran she probably deserved it anyway, bet she leads people on, just like you."

A red hot flame shot from my stomach into my head. It took over my brain and I lunged forward, my hands already clawed ready to grab his scrawny neck. Only Luke's arms wrapping around my waist and holding on tight, stopped me.

"Rachel, stop. That doesn't solve anything," he ordered.

"Yes it does," I hissed, struggling to get away from him. "It'll make me feel better." I tried to prize his fingers loose, but I'd got no chance, Luke was way too strong. "Let me go!"

Joshua blew a kiss then stood there with this great stupid grin on his face, making me even madder.

"Looks like these three came looking for trouble," he said.

Still struggling, I frowned. Who was he talking to?

"Looks like they've found it then." The voice came from behind us. I twisted to look over Luke's shoulder. Three of Joshua's mates had silently come up behind us and were standing with hands flexing and eyes bright with expectancy. The left one was short with his head shaved so close he was almost bald. Scars, I presume from previous battles covered his scalp. The middle one was tall and wiry, but had a confident stare with his mates beside him. The one on the right was beefy with muscles trying to rip their way out of his T-shirt. I wanted to believe that because two of us were girls they wouldn't do anything, but I knew better, that would never stop Joshua's gang.

CHAPTER TEN

I stopped struggling against Luke and felt his arms loosen their grip. I stared at the three thugs, my stomach bunching into a tight knot.

"Guess what lads, she wants me to confess," Joshua's voice rang with laughter.

"Confess to what?" Shorty grinned.

"She thinks I duffed up her gran," Joshua smirked. "Now, would I do summat like that?"

"You? Naw, you're such a good boy, you wouldn't do a nasty thing like that. Now, me, that sort of thing's right up my street." Beefy ground his left fist into his right palm.

"But me and Rachel have a score to settle, don't we, Rachel?" Joshua's brown eyes glinted. "Me and my guys have been a bit busy with '*things*' this last week …" Amused snorting came from behind me. "But now we've got time and were gonna come looking for you in the next couple of days. Nice of you to save us the trouble, isn't it guys?"

The knot in my stomach twisted impossibly tight as his mates grunted and jeered.

This was gonna be like, pay back for rejecting him and kneeing him in the groin. Obviously hurting Gran wasn't enough revenge for him.

"I reckon it's the boyfriend's fault," Joshua added, his eyes focusing on Luke, "If it wasn't for him there'd be no problem."

Luke's arm muscles flexed as my heart flipped over.

"It's *not* Luke's fault," I shouted, stepping towards Joshua, "I wouldn't fancy you if you were the last boy on the planct."

"Oh yeah?" Joshua's hand shot out and grabbed my right arm, pulling me towards him so sharply my arm twisted.

"Aargh!" I cried out in pain as his other arm wrapped around my waist and pulled me right up to him. I was crushed against his body, my heart racing so fast it felt like it would burst.

I tried to push away with my free arm but he was too strong and his grip on me tightened, squeezing me against him.

"Get off her!" I heard Luke shout, but he didn't get to me. I heard him grunt then groan, spitting air out of his lungs. I knew Joshua's mates had grabbed him and hit him.

Rage shot through my body like a fire, they couldn't hurt Luke, he hadn't done anything. I struggled against Joshua's grip, twisting and wriggling, trying to free myself from his grasp. My wrist and waist burned with pain as his grip tightened against my efforts. Finally I'd turned enough so that my back was to Joshua but he still held me tight. Luke was doubled up, obviously in pain. Wiry and Shorty each held one of his arms whilst Beefy pulled back his fist to hit Luke again.

"Let go of him!" I yelled. Rebecca lay on the ground, obviously knocked down by one of the thugs. She pushed herself up and launched herself at Beefy as his fist connected with Luke's stomach. Luke groaned in pain as Rebecca jumped on Beefy's back, scratching his face and squeezing her legs around his waist trying to kick him in the stomach. As Luke's knees buckled,

97

Beefy reached around and pulled Rebecca off like a rag doll throwing her back onto the ground.

Luke took his chance. His legs straightened and his muscles flexed. He threw Shorty off his right arm, then turned and thumped Wiry. Wiry was stronger than he looked and although he reeled from the blow he recovered quickly, throwing himself at Luke. Luke hit the ground with Wiry on top and Shorty lurching towards him.

I seemed to have been watching ages but it'd only been a few seconds. Beefy turned from Rebecca, who lay near the stone wall shaking her head like she was trying to clear it, and headed for Luke. I couldn't let them be three on one again. In desperation instinct took over. I raised my right foot and brought the heel down as hard as I could on Joshua's ankle. At the same time I dug my nails into his arms like a tiger clawing its prey. My nails sank deep into his skin.

"Aargh, you ...," but Joshua didn't get to finish. In his pain he'd loosened his grip and my left arm came free. Thinking fast, I slammed it backwards into his ribs with every bit of my strength. Joshua gasped and let me go. Immediately I jumped forward straight onto Beefy's back, just as Rebecca had done. Beefy's arms came around to pull me off, but I wrapped my arms around his neck and clung on. Rebecca staggered up, took a deep breath then bent double and raced forwards. She ploughed into Shorty just as he raised his foot to kick Luke. Luke safely rolled to his right still wrestling Wiry as Shorty toppled sideways with Rebecca on top of him.

Beefy's fingers suddenly clamped onto my right arm. Pain shot through it and I found myself flying through the air, torn off Beefy's back by his monster hands.

I landed hard on the ground, my lungs exploding as all the air crashed out of them. Rebecca rolled around the floor gouging Shorty's face. Beefy turned from me and headed for Luke. Joshua lurched towards my Luke as well, his forehead creased in a deep frown and his eyes filled with hatred. This had to stop, it was getting really bad.

Suddenly one of my brain cells woke up and I remembered my mobile. My eyes scanned the floor and spotted my bag near Rebecca's head. I scrambled up and keeping low so as not to attract attention, I crept forwards, dove for my bag and yanked it clear.

Fumbling for the zip, I edged backwards away from the battle, pulling and tugging at it. Why wouldn't the thing work? I was just ready for tearing the whole bag apart when finally the zip moved. I plunged my hand inside and rummaged around for my mobile. Finally my fingers closed around it and gripping it tightly with relief, I pulled it out and dialed 999.

I'd backed up against the wall and impatiently hopped from foot to foot as it rang. I wanted to get in there and help Luke. Wiry and Beefy had dragged him to his feet and Joshua was closing in, his fist raised.

"Come on!" I urged then almost cried with relief when a voice said.

"What service do you require?"

"Police please," I almost yelled.

Joshua's fist exploded into Luke's stomach and Luke doubled up, coughing, held up by the two thugs. Joshua was just lining up a second blow when I shouted again.

"Help, we're being attacked!"

Instead of hitting Luke, Joshua swung around towards me and ran. He would have my phone any

99

second and I hadn't told the police where we were. So I dropped it in the nearest, safest place I could think of ... down my cleavage. Well down the front of my top anyway.

At the same time I shouted, "We're at St Mary's church, Scarborough, come quick!"

Joshua reached me and frantically tried to rip my top out from my shorts while I desperately tried to keep it in there. A voice spoke from my stomach, asking for my name.

"It's Rachel Brooks," I yelled. "Come quick! Let go of me!"

I kicked out at Joshua but it went wild and missed completely.

Luke must've seen Joshua head for me because he suddenly had this burst of energy. He fiercely swung his right arm and threw Wiry off onto one of the grave stones which cracked loudly and broke in two. Then Luke turned on Beefy, his fist clenched tight and punched him right in the face. Beefy sort of, swayed and stumbled backwards, letting go of Luke's other arm. Suddenly free, Luke dove forward and ripped Joshua away from me.

"Leave Rachel alone, you freak!" he yelled.

"Can you tell me what is happening?" the muffled voice spoke from my stomach again.

I didn't want to answer, I wanted them to just shut up and come.

"Rachel, can you tell me what is happening?"

"Just come! They're attacking us!" I yelled, as Joshua managed to turn around and plant his fist in my Luke's face. "Leave him alone!" I yelled and threw myself at him. The impact made him stumble into Luke and we all fell. Luke picked himself up, but so did Joshua, Wiry and Beefy. With frowns deeper than the Grand Canyon they headed for Luke.

"There's four of them," I yelled, "They're attacking us. We're two girls and one boy and we need help NOW!"

By then Joshua was wrestling with Luke, Beefy and Wiry were closing in and even Shorty had thrown off Rebecca and was heading towards us. I whacked Joshua around the head with my bag, my top jiggling about so much the phone found a gap and slipped out onto the floor.

Faintly I heard the officer say, "A unit is already on their way."

I ignored it, balanced on my left foot and kicked the back of Joshua's right knee as hard as I could with my other foot. I couldn't believe my success as Joshua yelped and toppled backwards. I just managed to jump out of the way in time to avoid him crashing into me.

My eyes caught Luke's just as Beefy and Wiry bowled into him, sending him sprawling on top of Joshua. They bent and grabbed Luke, dragging him up as sirens filled the air. I've never been so relieved in all my life. The two thugs just froze like somebody'd pressed the 'pause' button with Luke hanging between them. Joshua scrambled to his feet, his head waggling wildly left to right, trying to figure out an escape route.

"Come on!" he yelled and sprinted off towards the top wall. Beefy, Shorty and Wiry came back to life and followed him, running like a stampede, across the grass.

A panda car screeched to a stop on Castle Road. Two policemen jumped out and leapt over the boundary wall. Another car pulled up next to the church and two officers ran across the grass, closing in behind Joshua and his gang preventing any escape. A third officer from the second car, walked calmly towards us.

Luke stood a metre away from me, doubled up with his hands resting on his knees.

"Are you okay?" I asked, bending beside him.

"Just about," he said, his breath coming in short gasps.

I slipped my arm around his shoulders.

"Don't anybody bother about me." Rebecca was also bent double, gasping for breath.

"Are you okay?" I asked, looking up without letting go of Luke.

"Getting there," she answered. "Did we win?"

"I think the police did," I answered.

"Can anyone tell me what happened here?" The policeman asked when he reached us. "Which one of you is Rachel?"

"I am," I said.

We gave them a rough outline, but of course, Joshua and his mates gave a completely different story so we all had to go to the police station.

We sat on plastic chairs, facing a reception counter with a six foot something police officer behind it. Every so often he turned and frowned at us, but other than that we were left alone. We'd all given our statements and been asked to wait. I looked across at Luke. His face was white other than a shiner developing around his right eye. He looked pinched and strained.

"Are you okay?" I whispered. I don't know why I whispered but it just felt right, like we were in church or something.

Luke shook his head.

"Are you in pain?"

"My ribs are killing me but that's not the problem," Luke murmured. He sat slouched, his elbows on his lap and his head resting on his hands, looking down at the floor between his knees. "This is *so* bad."

"Why? It wasn't our fault."

"Wasn't it?" Luke lifted his head, a really weird look on his face.

"No," I said. Where was he coming from? "Of course it wasn't our fault, they attacked us. Remember?"

"No, I don't. We were the ones who went and threatened Joshua, saying we'd turn him in if he didn't turn himself in. And he only grabbed you when you went for him."

"Luke?" I couldn't believe I was hearing this. "Are you trying to say all this is my fault?"

"No." He paused. "But the police might think it is, especially if they listen to Joshua's version."

"But he's lying." If I wasn't in the police station I would've been on my feet waving my arms about in exasperation but I couldn't, so I just gritted my teeth.

"But they don't know that," Luke said, his eyes fixed back on the floor again. "What if they believe him? Or at least, what if they doubt us?"

"Well they can't prove anything either way, so we're okay. Anyway, it's not like we did any major damage to them or they to us, so it'll be no big deal."

Luke's shoulders slumped, "It is to me."

"Why?" I couldn't figure what had gotten into him, he was fine when it was all happening, so why was he stressing now?

"You don't get it, do you?" He lifted his head again and his beautiful blue eyes met mine. My stomach turned over when I saw the fear deep inside them. "I'm on my last warning. When I hit Carl, the guy who'd been bullying me for years, the judge let me off but said if I got in trouble again he'd lock me up. Remember? Can't you see? If the police check all our records they'll see I'm on a warning, they'll probably believe Joshua and lock me up."

"Why did they threaten to lock you up just for hitting a bully?" Rebecca sat forward in her seat. I looked across at her.

"Because he used a baseball bat," I said.

Rebecca's eyebrows raised. "Oh, yeah, that'd do it," she said and sat back in her seat.

"He didn't plan it," I said, I couldn't have her thinking Luke was some crazy lunatic or something. "Carl cornered him. The bat was just there."

Rebecca shrugged. "Whatever. The bully probably deserved it."

"No one deserves to be hit by a baseball bat," Luke said quietly, without looking up.

Rebecca just shrugged.

Just then a door opened next to the reception desk and a policeman came out with a bunch of A4 papers in his hand.

"All right, we've contacted your parents or guardians," he looked at me. "By their agreement, a Mr Wintoga is coming to collect you," he said. "Once he arrives, you are free to go."

"Is that it then?" Rebecca asked.

'Shut up!' I shouted in my head. I just wanted to get Luke out of there before they changed their minds.

"Yes, that's all for now. We have your statements and your addresses."

The 'for now' made my heart flutter.

"What about Joshua and his gang?" I asked.

"They will be released shortly."

I gasped. "But they attacked us. They hurt my gran." I couldn't believe this, how could they let them go? I'd told them all about my suspicions when I was interviewed. This was the chance they needed to get Joshua locked up for good.

"We have no evidence regarding your grandmother's mugging, I'm afraid. Unless your grandmother can identify her attacker there is nothing we can do. I understand she is unable to do that."

"She's too scared to," I said, a burning sensation in my chest. "But if he's locked up she might have the courage to tell us about it, or identify him."

The policeman shook his head. "It doesn't work that way, I'm afraid. We have already spoken to your grandmother, she says she cannot identify the boy and does not wish to come down here. Now, we will deal with Joshua and his friends regarding this incident, but that is all we can do at this time."

"Don't you see? She won't come because she's scared! She hasn't left the bungalow since he attacked her. You've got to do something!" I couldn't believe this, I'd handed Joshua to them and they still weren't doing anything. I felt like grabbing him, shaking him, making him see sense.

The officer shook his head. "I'm afraid there's nothing we can do. In the absence of other witnesses, if your grandmother cannot identify her assailant then our hands are tied."

I bit my lip, hard. This was hopeless. I'd tried to help, but it had gone completely wrong. Luke was hurt and our parents informed. They'd probably whisk us home before our feet crossed Gran's doorstep. And worse, Joshua was free and would hate me even more now. He'd be out for revenge. None of us would be safe. A finger of ice slid down my spine. In just two more weeks Gran would be on her own and that's only if Mum and Dad didn't demand I go straight home. She'd never go out again and if she did, anything could happen.

CHAPTER ELEVEN

Mr Wintoga drove us to Gran's in silence, I think he was secretly grateful he'd taken Sam out for the day so she hadn't been dragged into trouble with us.

My stomach somersaulted at the thought of facing Gran and I know Rebecca and Luke were worrying about the inevitable phone calls from their parents. But, like, if we were all sent straight home, what'd happen to Gran?

"We ought to get you checked at the hospital," I finally said when we were nearly there.

"No, it doesn't hurt as much now, I'll just get cleaned up, that's all."

"But what about your eye? It's half closed."

Luke shrugged. "I've had black eyes before. Had them all the time when Carl and his gang were beating up on me. Compared to the others, this isn't bad."

"But what about your ribs?" I couldn't believe he was being so casual about all this. He looked a mess.

"They're bruised, not broken. I've had plenty battered ribs before as well. Look, stop worrying, if I needed the hospital I'd go, okay?"

I stared at Luke, he'd never snapped at me before.

"Are you okay?" I asked.

Luke frowned. "I said I was."

I backed off, chewing my thumb, this wasn't the Luke I knew, something was definitely wrong. I decided to try again.

"I mean, you, not the injuries. Are *you* all right?" I said, softly.

Luke tilted his head back, staring up at the roof of the car, his hands deep in his pockets. He took a deep breath then said, almost in a whisper.

"Look, it just ... brought too much back, okay? I hated it, not being able to help you and Rebecca. I felt useless just like I did all those years when I was bullied at my old school. It didn't matter how strong I got from doing sports they were always stronger, just like today. Then in the police station, I was like, so scared, I still am. I've had my final warning. There's still a chance they'll look at my record and believe Joshua. I could get locked up, I couldn't handle that and it'd kill Mum to have me inside as well as Matt."

"That's not gonna happen," I said, trying to sound more confident than I felt.

All this stuff with Gran and Joshua, the crazy lunatic nurse and now Luke, I was like, way out of my depth. I just wished I could figure out how to make everything right for everybody.

"How do you know?" Luke asked.

My brain raced, trying to find a convincing answer.

"Because, if they were gonna lock you up they'd have done it while we were there. I mean, there's no way they'd have let us go before checking up on us all. They must've seen the circumstances of your arrest and realised it wasn't your fault."

"It was my fault."

I almost growled with frustration.

"You were provoked, you were bullied into it, I mean, come on, the creep broke your arm! The judge understood that, that's why you only got rep ... rep ... community service."

108

"Reparation."

"Ugh?"

"Reparation, that's what it's called."

I sighed, I didn't really care what it was called I was in the middle of making a point.

"Whatever. Anyway, the judge saw that and today the police could see there were four onto three and two of us are lasses. It's obvious who was at fault. And I'm the one who called for help, remember? I mean, I'm not likely to do that if we were the ones causing trouble, am I? Look, don't worry about it. I'm telling you, it'll be all right."

Luke looked at me. "You reckon?"

I nodded, wishing I was really convinced. We were already on Gran's road and I watched her bungalow come into view. I thanked Mr Wintoga and opened the door just as Luke's mobile rang. He groaned and snapped it open.

"Oh, yeah, hi Mum," he grimaced and walked down the road a little, talking quietly. I could see by his posture and arm movements that things were not going well. Finally he snapped the mobile shut, his shoulders slumped.

"What did she say?" I asked, as he walked back to us.

Luke shook his head. "She was freaking out. She's like 'you're going to end up in prison like your brother. I can't handle that. You'll have to come home.'"

My eyes widened. "You're not, are you?"

Luke shook his head, "No, I managed to talk her round. But if there's even the slightest sniff of any more trouble I'm on the next train out of here."

Phew. My whole body sighed, deflating like a balloon. I hadn't realised I'd been holding my breath.

109

"I'm glad you can stay," I said, wrapping my arms around his neck. As we kissed, Rebecca's phone rang. We separated and watched her glance at it and groan.

"My turn," she muttered and wandered off further up the road while Luke and I watched, our arms around each other's waists.

After a couple of minutes she walked back to us, grinning.

"What did she say?" I asked.

"I can stay."

"Why, what did you tell her?" She looked so laid back about it all, I couldn't believe it.

"I told her that a lad touched you up, we went to talk to him about it and his gang had a go at us. The only sticky bit was being here with you. I'm supposed to be here with friends, but the police told Mum I was with my sister. You can imagine how well that went down, I haven't even told her we've found each other yet."

"Are your parents still arguing about whether you should know about Rachel?" Luke asked, frowning.

Rebecca rolled her eyes. "Since they split up they're arguing about everything. Mum always said I should know and told me. But it was our secret because Dad disagreed. He'd go mental if he found out me and Rach are in contact. He'd figure Mum went behind his back and they'd have something else to argue about. So I kept it a secret. Anyway, Mum's cool about us being together once I'd explained everything. She's just not gonna tell Dad anything."

I smiled but then my stomach sank.

"Now it's my turn." I took a deep breath and opened Gran's gate.

Gran started as soon as I walked in. She totally ignored Rebecca and Luke and just went off on one.

"Rachel, just what did you think you were doing?" She demanded. I opened my mouth to defend myself but Gran didn't pause for breath. "I couldn't believe it when the police rang. After all I've been through. Have you any idea how I felt? I thought you'd been hurt. They were going to ring your Mother."

My heart actually skipped a beat with hope, but sagged again as Gran continued.

"I had to tell them your parents are away on holiday and that I'd tell them as soon as they return. Now I'm lying to the police. You know I don't want your parents fussing around. You young people today just go and behave like hooligans and don't care about old people like me."

I could see her eyes watering and felt like the lowest form of life on the planet. What had I done?

"If it wasn't for ..." Gran's jaw tensed but she didn't finish the sentence. "I would send you straight home." She blinked quickly.

"I'm sorry, Gran," I managed to squeak out through my straw-like throat. I'd never felt so bad.

"And who is this Joshua boy you confronted?" Gran crossed her arms, looking like a sergeant major.

"We think he's the one who hurt you," I said, my voice barely more than a whisper.

"So the police said," Gran snapped, "And how are you to know that when I haven't described him? The police only wanted me to go down there and look at pictures! I'm just not up to that and what's the point if I don't know what he looks like? Having a name doesn't help, he didn't take time to introduce himself. Now you leave this Joshua boy alone. You hear me?"

111

Gran's face was getting whiter by the second. It was so obvious she was terrified of him.

"But Gran …"

"Just go to your room. Both of you," she said, wafting me away. She turned to Luke. "They will see you tomorrow."

I looked up at Luke, my eyes telling him how sorry I was. His one good eye and the bruised one looked back at me, telling me he understood. Then he turned but just as the door closed, he smiled and winked, leaving a warm ember glowing in my heart.

"Look, Gran..." I started, but she held up her hand.

"Just go!" She snapped.

The ember flickered out, my head dropped and I dragged myself into my bedroom. Rebecca followed and closed the door behind us.

"Wow, that was tense," she murmured.

I dropped onto the bed and looked up at her, my eyes filling with tears.

"Can you blame her? After what she's been through, all I do is go and bring more trouble. I thought I was helping. I so wanted to help!"

My chin crumbled and I lost the battle as tears ran down my cheeks.

"What have I done? I've made it loads worse! Now Joshua's really gonna be out for Gran and I'll not be here to look after her!"

Rebecca came over, sat down beside me and put her arms around my shaking shoulders.

"Look, you're not due home for a couple of weeks. We've got time. We'll think of summat."

I looked into her intense brown eyes.

"Like what?"

"Hey, I don't know, but we've got time to think about it," she said with a shrug.

Why didn't anything bother Rebecca? She was so laid back it was unreal. If we didn't look alike I'd never believe we were twins.

***

The next morning I woke up and stretched, then the events of the day before came back to me and I groaned. I wished I could go back, start the day again and do everything differently. I definitely wouldn't go looking for Joshua!

I sat up and glanced down at Rebecca's bed, it was empty.

Yawning I walked out into the hall. Pots clattered in the kitchen and bath water rain noisily down the drain in the bathroom. Wandering into the sitting room and over to the window, I tweeked the curtain aside to check the weather and my breath caught.

"I don't believe it," I gasped.

"What?" Rebecca's voice came from behind me. I glanced at her as she came over, already in jeans and blue T-shirt and rubbing her wet hair with a towel.

"She's back."

"Who?" Rebecca's eyes were glazed over, not fully awake even after her bath.

"The physco nurse," I hissed, like I was scared she'd hear me. I mean, as if, she was like, 20 metres away, standing half hidden behind a lamp post. I could just see her baggy blue cardigan and blue trousers.

"Let me see."

Rebecca nudged me out of the way and stuck her head around the curtain.

113

"What *is* her problem?" she said, her hands heading for her hips.

"She's weird or something," I said. "Like, as if I haven't got enough trouble with Joshua, the police and Gran, without *her*."

"Do you want me to sort her out?"

"No! She could be psycho and she'd think you're me."

"Exactly." Rebecca's hands had reached her hips and were jammed in place, the towel limply hanging from her right hand. "I'll do what you're too scared to do. I'll tell her to get lost and go haunt somebody else."

"I'm not scared." I lifted my chin. No way was I gonna let her think I was scared. Because I wasn't. Well, not much, not really. Well actually I was pretty freaked out, but I wasn't gonna let Rebecca know that. "I'm just sensible," I said, "She could be an axe murderer or something."

"Oh, yeah," Rebecca said, smirking. "You said that before, but I don't see an axe. I mean, where is it? Stuck down her trousers or hidden inside that baggy cardy?"

"Might be."

"Yeah, sure."

"Okay, go talk to her if you want, but be careful, all right?"

Rebecca nodded.

"And don't be too rude, I don't want her coming after me."

Rebecca rolled her eyes, turned and left the room.

I heard the front door open and click shut then watched Rebecca walk out onto the street. She turned left and headed for the nurse, who spotted her and stiffened but stayed put.

My heart pounded. I felt so guilty, I should've gone with Rebecca. I mean, what if the nurse did something? Rebecca was all alone. I felt like the worse coward ever. But one thing I knew, pyjamas or not, if that woman tried to hurt Rebecca, I'd be out that door faster than a tongue on a hot date.

I watched Rebecca reach the nurse. She stood half a metre from her, hands on hips, her head bobbing up and down like she was telling the nurse where to get off.

The nurse said something, frowning a bit, her arms out like she was pleading or something. I stared, wishing I could read lips.

Suddenly Rebecca stiffened then snapped forwards, leaning in towards the nurse, jabbing her finger at her like she was giving her a right telling off. Then her arm shot out sideways, pointing away.

The nurse shook her head, leaning toward Rebecca, her arms out further like she was begging.

Curiosity was killing me, I wished I was dressed and could go hear what was happening. She didn't look like a pyscho now, she looked more like she was desperate or something.

Rebecca jabbed her arm away again, she was shouting now, but all I could hear were muffled voices. I wished my ears were receivers or something I could just tune in to listen. I couldn't wait any more. I raced to the bedroom, pulled off my pjs, flung open my case and grabbed the first jeans and top I could lay my hands on. Pulling them on, I headed out into the hall, hopping as I tried to get the second leg into the jeans.

I'd just succeeded and reached the front door when it flung wide, nearly hitting me in the face. Rebecca stormed in, her face bright red, her lips so thin they'd almost disappeared.

"What happened?" I asked, as she barged past me.

Pulling up my zip, I followed her into the sitting room.

She paced backwards and forwards between the settee and the chairs for longer than I could stand.

"Rebecca! What happened?"

"That woman," she said, shaking her head and pointing at the window. "That woman. Just who does she think she is? Thinks she can throw us away then just pick us back up again when she wants!"

I froze. Had I really just heard what I thought I'd heard? My breath wouldn't come. I just stood there, watching Rebecca pace. My chest hurt and my head felt really light, like it would float away.

"She's our mother?" I managed to whisper.

"NO!" Rebecca glared at me, like I'd just insulted her. "She's *not* our mother. We have mothers. Women who've been there for us, that's what a mother is."

Suddenly coming back to life, I sprang forwards and grabbed Rebecca's arms, shaking her as I spoke.

"Is.she.our.mother?"

"No." Rebecca's voice was flat.

"Rebecca?" I stared into her eyes, trying to read her mind or hypnotise her into telling the truth. "Is she our birth mother?"

"If that's what you want to call it."

My arms dropped.

"She's our birth mother and you let her go?" I turned away from her, I couldn't look at her.

"She's nothing."

I spun back. My blood boiling.

"Rebecca, she's our birth mother and you sent her away! How could you? You know how much I wanted to find her!"

"Oh, yeah and that's why you've spent hours searching for her!" Rebecca was almost snarling, her voice so vicious.

I gasped, I couldn't believe she was being like this.

"I spent all my time looking for you. After I found you, there were no clues to Mum or Dad, but you know I wanted to find them."

"She was a psycho a few minutes ago." Rebecca glared at me.

"That's before I knew who she was."

"She's still a psycho. Do you know, the only reason she's in Scarborough is because she found out you lived here? She was too late to find you but she's asked around and found out about your Gran. She's been watching her ever since, hoping you'd come back and visit. She was real happy when your Gran got mugged and you turned up at the hospital. Compassionate or what?"

I felt real wobbly like my legs had gone all soft.

"She's been trying to find me?"

"Us. She's been trying to find both of us. Like we'd want anything to do with her?"

"But I do!" This was too much, way too much. "Did she think you were me?"

Rebecca snorted again. "Yeah, well that was the whole idea, wasn't it? That I get rid of her so she won't bother you anymore. Well, that's what I did. She was too busy begging and pleading to notice my hair's shorter."

My lungs didn't have enough air in them. It was like the life had been sucked out of me.

"She thinks I sent her away," I whispered.

A thought suddenly struck me, energy sweeping back in.

"Where did she go?"

"Away." Rebecca thrust her hands into her pockets, her head down.

"Where?"

"How should I know?"

I clenched my teeth. "Which way did she go?"

Rebecca shrugged.

"Pscch!" I sucked in air, too angry to say any more. Instead I turned and marched out of the room, down the hall and out of the front door. Once outside I looked right and left. I had to find her, but which way?

CHAPTER TWELVE

After a bit of neck straining, I could see well down the road on my left, but she wasn't there so I turned right. At the end of the road, I looked both ways along Wykeham Street. She could've turned right and already gone over the bridge or turned left and gone down St John's Road so she'd be out of sight. This was hopeless, I mean, she might even have come in a car and already be long gone. Running to the right I reached the top of the bridge but apart from a couple of young kids dancing about, there was no-one. I bit my lip, my chest tight. I couldn't miss her now, I just couldn't. The thought of her walking away, thinking I hated her and didn't want to see her made me ache inside. It was so not true. I wanted to see her more than anything to find out who I was. Suddenly making up my mind, I spun around and charged back the way I came. I passed Gran's Street and turned onto St John's Road. The street was quiet and I could hear my feet pounding on the pavement, my breath coming in short bursts as I ran.

I knew it was hopeless, I was too late, there were so many ways she could have gone, but I wasn't thinking straight. It was like I'd lost her all over again.

I reached Hampton Road and decided to try that, there was a bend in the road, she could be just around it. By now tears were coursing down my cheeks, I could feel the breeze stinging and drying them as I raced. I panted as my legs screamed for me to stop. My chest hurt but something drove me on. It was like I was manic or something. I just had to find her.

I raced past parked cars and bay windows, hardly noticing anything, just frantically searching for her but she was nowhere in sight. I rounded the bend in the road staring ahead, standing on tip toes to see over the cars, but there was nothing. I ran on.

Finally I had to give in and doubled over, my left side burning. I held onto it, grimacing with pain. My chest felt like it was being squeezed as I gasped for breath. Somewhere in the distance I could hear Rebecca shouting my name, but I didn't answer.

It was a good ten minutes before my breathing settled down and my heart rate returned to it's normal thump, thump. Straightening up, I turned back towards Gran's. I'd only walked a few metres when I realised what an idiot I'd been. I stopped sharp and shook my head. I'd been speeding around the streets like a lunatic, panicking that I'd never see her again when all along I knew exactly where to find her. I couldn't believe I'd forgotten. The hospital. She'd actually been wearing her uniform, the blue trousers and blue cardy, I bet that was covering the white nurses' tunic! I set off again, walking slowly back to Gran's. Later I'd go to the hospital and meet my mother. I was gonna find out everything about her and why she threw us away all those years ago. By the end of the day I'd know who I really was.

I spotted Rebecca walking towards me and slowed down even more, sticking my hands in my pockets.

"Rachel, I'm sorry." She stopped right in front of me, blocking my way.

I stared down at my trainers.

"No, really, I am sorry. Look, you know how I feel about our birth parents for dumping us. I've always been straight about that. Well, when she told me who she was, I like, freaked. I shouldn't have let her think I was you. I should've told her who I was and that I didn't want to see her but you might. But, like, I didn't have chance to think, you know, it just, like, happened."

I'd never heard Rebecca so unsure of herself before. I looked up and she had this like, little worried frown and her shoulders were slumped. I'm so soft, I just couldn't stay mad at her anymore, especially since I'd figured out how I was gonna see my birth mother again.

"It's okay," I said, "I'll sort it."

Rebecca smiled, her shoulders lifting.

"So, what're we doing today?" She was back to her old self again. I wish I could recover from things so quickly.

"Well, I wondered ..."

"If I'd stay and look after your gran for a bit and do my own thing, so you and Luke could go out and have a snog on the beach."

"Rebecca!" I hissed, looking round to make sure nobody heard. "We won't be snogging on the beach!"

"But you will be snogging," she said with a grin.

I smiled, feeling the stress seeping out of me. "We might."

"Knew it," she said and linked her arm in mine. "Come on then, let's get some breakfast then tart you up ready for a sexy date with your man."

I shook my head. Sometimes you just didn't argue with Rebecca, it was better to just ignore her and do you own thing anyway.

I texted Luke and at ten o'clock he knocked on Gran's door. He looked loads better although his shiner was glowing.

I grinned.

"Shall I put some purple eye shadow on your other eye so they match?" I asked.

Luke just gave me a look that said, 'Try and you die.'

He looked over my shoulder. "Are we going out on our own?"

"Yes." Rebecca's head appeared around the kitchen doorway. "I know when I'm not wanted. You too Love Birds go off and have your fun without me."

My stomach twisted with guilt.

"You can come if you want," I said.

Rebecca raised her eyebrows, "What? And miss an exciting game of scrabble with your gran? I've heard about her cheating, so I'm gonna see it as a challenge to thoroughly trounce her."

"I heard that," Gran's voice came from the sitting room. "And I do not cheat. It is you young ones who are not educated and if anyone will be doing any trouncing it will be me."

Rebecca grinned and winked. "See you later."

"See you," I said and stepped outside with Luke.

As we walked down to the sea front, I asked him about his injuries, then told him about my birth mother.

"Wow. With all that's going on that's the last thing you need. Or is it? How do you feel about it?"

I shrugged. "I don't know really. I mean, it's the last thing I expected. I'd given up on ever seeing my parents and for it to happen now ... As if I haven't got enough to deal with, you know, with Joshua and Gran. But I like, can't ignore it. I mean, she knows my family background and everything. She can tell me who I am."

"You already know who you are." Luke stopped walking and looked down at me, his hands on my shoulders. "You're funny, loving, *stressing* but

122

beautiful, Rachel Brooks. Knowing about her doesn't alter anything. You are who you are."

I sighed, looking up into those blue eyes, like deep pools I could just swim in forever. It was so hard to think straight when Luke was around.

"I know, it's just that, since I found out I was adopted there's been these questions in my head and now I've found her I can get some answers. Anyway, even if she can't tell me much, she can tell me why she gave me up. Me and Rebecca, I mean. Like, why didn't she have us adopted or anything legal? Why did she just abandon us? I have to know. And did she just like, walk away or did she hang around to make sure somebody found us? It's important."

Luke nodded. "Yeah, I get it. Do you want me to come with you?"

I shook my head. "No, I'd rather go on my own."

We'd reached the sea front by then and stopped at the first hot dog stand we came to. It was set in the wall between noisy amusement arcades, the sound and smell of sizzling sausages wafting out.

Luke had one with onions and ketchup. I just had brown sauce with mine.

We walked across the road at the next crossing and found an unoccupied bench. We climbed on and sat on the back, our feet resting on the seat. Here at the front it was pretty cold in the sea breeze, but there were still plenty of families on the beach. Parents sheltered behind wind breakers while kids with their trousers rolled up played in the sand. There were even a few crazies swimming in the sea. Just the thought of it made me shiver and I snuggled up to Luke. I wrapped the paper tight around my hot dog to keep it warm, tilting my head to take a bite without the sauce squirting

123

out. Luke did the same, holding his in both hands and for a short time my problems were forgotten. I was safe here with Luke, warm next to his firm body. Once the hot dogs were gone, he wrapped his arm around my shoulders drawing me further in. I could have stayed there forever, hearing the waves in the distance across the sand, laughter and bleeping amusements behind us. It was like our little bit of heaven, just for me and Luke. I sighed and wrapped my arm around his waist. It felt so good. Why couldn't my whole stay here be this good?

"Hey, look who's there!" Ruby's voice broke my reverie.

"Hi, Rube," I said, turning to see three of my friends heading towards us. "Where's Sam?"

"Out with her family again," said Summer. She stepped right in front of us, her eyes traveling over Luke's body. "So this is Luke?"

"Yeah. Luke, this is Summer, Ruby and Ruby's sister, Sapphire."

"Hi," Luke nodded.

Ruby's eyes sparkled.

"You're right Rach, he's definitely hot."

"Ruby!" I felt my cheeks burn despite the cold and when I looked at Luke his cheeks were definitely pinker than they were a few minutes ago as well.

Summer licked her lips slowly, sexily.

"Yeah, you're definitely hot. If you ever get fed up with Rachel ..."

"Hands off! He's mine!" I said, giving her a friendly thump.

"That black eye just makes him sexier," came a quiet voice.

"Sapphire!" We all shouted together. Sapphire's little face peeked out from behind Ruby, her cheeks rosy. I think she'd surprised herself as well as us, but there was also a mischievous, defiant look I'd never seen before.

We all stared open-mouthed then burst out laughing, even Luke.

They stayed and chatted for a while before heading off towards a chip stand.

"Don't do anything I wouldn't do!" Ruby called as they left.

"That doesn't give me many limitations!" I called after her and got a finger as answer.

Feeling colder now, we walked along the front our arms around each other's waists, dodging push chairs and squealing kids.

"Nice friends," Luke said.

"Yeah, I miss them when I'm in Rotherham," I said. "Sam's great too, you'll like her."

We talked about everything and anything and every now and again we stopped and kissed. I didn't want the morning to end, but after a bit I started to feel guilty about Gran. I was supposed to be here to see her and I'd left Rebecca doing my job. Knowing I wanted to go to the hospital in the afternoon, I knew I had to put in an appearance.

"Do you want to come to Gran's for dinner?" I asked, hoping for the right answer.

"You cooking?" Luke asked.

"Yep," I answered.

"Then no, I'll find a cafe." Luke grinned and got a thump on the arm. "Oy," he said, looking wounded. "I'm still injured, you know."

"Yeah, well, watch it, or you'll end up worse."

"Ooo, big threats. I suppose I'd better say, 'yes' then."

"That's better," I said and squeezed his arm.

I texted Rebecca that I'd cook dinner, then called at the shops on the way back and bought extra veg.

As the bungalow came into sight, my stomach flipped over and my happy mood evaporated. It was all still here, reality. Gran healed on the outside but not on the inside, afraid to go out. Joshua, getting away with it and the nurse, my birth mother who gave me the creeps but who I'd got to go see. My arm tightened around Luke.

"You okay?" He looked down at me, his eyes filled with concern.

I nodded. "I just wish everything was okay, like it used to be."

"It will be again," he said and kissed my head.

I didn't really believe him, I mean, how could he know? But I was grateful to him for trying to comfort me. I managed a weak smile.

"After dinner," he said, "Let me know if you want me to come to the hospital with you."

I nodded. "Yeah, thanks."

But I knew I wouldn't, I'd no idea how the meeting would go and I didn't want anybody there, not even Luke.

We reached Gran's and I stretched a smile across my face. I had to look cheerful for her, somehow we'd got to get her feeling good again.

***

After dinner I left Rebecca and Luke washing up with Gran and caught a bus to the hospital. I'd timed my arrival for visiting time so nobody would question me being there.

It felt surreal as I approached the same entrance I'd used when visiting Gran. The yellow overhang with

126

ambulance parking bays on both sides made my stomach flip over. The fear for Gran was still so strong but now this place held the secret of my past as well, inside the head of a phsyco nurse I'd been running from until now.

I walked in through the glass doors, my eyes scanning the A & E for nurses' uniforms. There were a couple but neither was the one I wanted. My heart suddenly dropped, I was so stupid. Where would I find her? It was a huge hospital and just because she was in her uniform earlier didn't mean anything, she could've just finished a shift. I'd got no way of finding out. I mean, what was I supposed to do, go up to someone and ask for the stalker nurse? Yeah, like that'd get me thrown out before I could blink.

I stood there like an idiot in the middle of A & E with nurses and visitors walking right past me, trying to figure out what to do.

Eventually I decided to look in each ward, hoping to spot her somewhere. I walked with my head up, hands tightly grasping my shoulder bag for comfort hoping anybody noticing me would figure I knew where I was going and leave me to my search.

Having seen the nurse near the Medical Admissions Unit when Gran was a patient, I decided to start there. I knew the route well now and was soon squirting my hands from the antiseptic dispenser. I headed into the ward and walked all the way up looking into each of the bays. I spotted one nurse and two health care assistants in their purple uniforms but not the psycho. Part of me wanted to stop thinking of her like that, I mean, she was like, my birth mother. But somehow I didn't want to attach the word 'mother' to her, it was like, too personal and I didn't want to feel that close.

Sighing I pushed open the doors and went back out into the corridor. The Coronary Care Unit was nearby so I turned that way and froze. She was there, the nurse, the birth mother, just stepping out of the Coronary Care Unit with a tall thin health care assistant. They were chatting and hadn't spotted me yet. I forced myself to breathe, watching her turn in my direction. It was like slow motion, I saw her every expression. She was smiling, talking, then her eyes widened along with her mouth. After that she stopped moving, like a still life we'd been studying in art just before the hols. The tall assistant, carried on walking and talking, then realised her friend had stopped. She looked back at birth mother, (BM sounds better), then followed her gaze to me.

I heard her ask if BM was okay. She got a nod for an answer and a waft of a hand shooing her away. She took the hint and carried on towards me, staring at me like I was some sort of alien or something.

Me and BM were on freeze frame until the tapping of the assistant's shoes faded and eventually died, leaving us alone.

"Rachel," BM said breathily. "I, I didn't think you wanted to see me again?"

I stared at her, taking in every detail again, but this time knowing she was my mother. Her hair had once been the same colour as mine before grey took hold, her brown eyes were the same and her nose turned up just like mine. I hated my nose but somehow it suited her face. This was so weird.

"That was my twin, Rebecca," I said, at last.

She gasped, her right hand shooting to her mouth. She sort of swayed a bit, then rested her left hand on the wall for support.

"You're both here," she whispered.

128

I nodded, hardly able to hear her for the distance. I knew I should move closer but somehow my legs wouldn't work. It was like I'd turned to stone except for my heart. That was working overtime, booming in my chest like a pneumatic drill.

BM shook her head, "And I never knew. You're so alike."

She stood straight again and began slowly walking towards me, looking me over like she was examining every part. "You have longer hair."

I nodded again. I'd gone, like, totally mute. I just didn't know what to say. This woman was my birth mother and I couldn't think of a word to say to her.

"She said ... she said you didn't want to see me." BM stood in front of me now.

Part of me felt like running away from her, but I shook my head, forcing myself to stay put. "I didn't know who you were, I thought you were just, er, well, you were following me."

"You thought I was a stalker. It must have seemed that way."

She was still staring at me, her eyes raking over my face. I looked down at my feet, my face burning.

"I'm sorry for staring," she said, "It's just that, you're the image of me at the same age."

I looked up, returning her stare now, wondering whether I'd look like her eventually. I hoped not. She seemed old beyond her years. I didn't know what to say. I felt like a tongue-tied idiot. This was so weird, I mean, for all I knew she could still be a psycho, she did abandon us as babies on the steps of Doncaster Hospital. That's not exactly normal behaviour, is it?

"I have half an hour break now. I was just going to the café. Do you want to join me? We could talk," she asked, her eyes wide with hope.

Part of me wanted to say 'No' and walk away, but another part couldn't, it was like a magnet drawing me to her. I nodded then followed her down echoing corridors to the café.

Once there BM bought us each a coke and led me to an empty table.

I sat down, the chair scraping across the floor. I tucked my legs under it and crossed my ankles tightly. She sat opposite staring at me again. I just wished she'd stop.

"I'm sorry to keep staring but I've waited so long for this moment. I never really thought it would come." Her face was all lit up like a kid in a sweet shop. "How are you? Are you happy? Well? How did you find your sister?" Her head dropped. "I heard you were adopted separately, I never wanted that."

'No, but you wanted us out of your life!' The words shouted in my brain but didn't find their way to my tongue.

Instead I heard myself saying, "I'm fine, so's Rebecca. It was hard finding her, but a few people with the right connections helped, they shouldn't have, but I'm glad they did."

I didn't want to tell her the details of my search, it was too personal and I didn't know her yet.

"I'm so glad you found each other and you're both happy and safe. That's all I ever wanted for you," she said, swallowing hard like she'd got a log in her throat.

A baby squealed across the room, drowning out the scraping of cutlery and soft conversation from other tables. I looked around making sure nobody was looking at us. BM's mood had changed so fast and the last thing I wanted was to sit here with a woman bawling her eyes out. She blinked rapidly then took a deep breath and began talking.

"I'm so sorry I couldn't keep you. I didn't want to give you up."

'Then why did you?' My heart screamed.

BM sighed heavily. "I owe you an explanation."

'Yes you do.' I thought but kept my lips clamped shut.

"I have a son, Mark. He was three when I got caught with you two."

I swallowed. I'd got an older brother. All my life I'd wished for a brother or sister and all this time I'd got both and never knew it.

She dropped her eyes like she'd said something wrong.

"I mean, I'd planned to have more children, sometime. Well, I'd hoped I would, but my Jed, well, he wasn't that stuck on kids. He'd not said much about Mark, maybe because he was a boy, I don't know. He never spent any time with him. When I found out I was pregnant, I was terrified." She twirled the glass around in her fingers glancing from side to side, making sure no-one could hear her I suppose. "You see, my Jed, he was, well, he was violent. If he didn't like something he'd hit first and think later. I was so scared I hid my pregnancy, wore loose clothes and everything. I didn't even go to a doctor, but you can't hide that sort of thing forever. We were in bed one night when he realised. It was terrible. He yelled and threatened, told me to get rid of you."

I stared at her. I'd never given abortion much thought before, but what if she'd done it? I might never

131

have existed ... A rush of cold swept through me and I shivered.

"But I said 'no'," BM continued, closing her eyes. "I'd never said 'no' to him before ..."

She stared down at her glass, the noises in the cafeteria fading. Finally she spoke again.

"I've never known rage like it. He hit me so hard I felt my cheek bone crack." She raised her hand to her left cheek. "I tried to get out of his way, but although he was a big man he was fast. I couldn't escape. He rained down blow after blow, all over my body. I tried to protect my stomach, curling around it so he couldn't hurt you." She glanced up at me then back down again. "I could feel blood running down my face, it ran into my eyes, but through the blur I could see young Mark. My little boy stood in the bedroom doorway and watched it all. I pleaded with Jed to stop, but he didn't. Jed kicked me until I lost consciousness. I don't know how long I was out, but I woke to find Mark sitting on the floor beside me, stroking me, his little face soaked in tears. Every part of me screamed with pain. I was convinced I'd lose you."

I stared open-mouthed at this woman, hardly believing this could be true. I couldn't see her face, but knew she was crying at the memory. Part of me wanted to get up and away from this embarrassing woman and another part wanted to reach out and touch her, to comfort her, but then, I didn't know her, she was a stranger to me. I couldn't do it. Instead I just sat there, gripping my glass so hard it's a wonder it didn't shatter. I wanted to know what happened, but here in the café?

"Why didn't you leave him?" I whispered.

She lifted her hand and wiped her eyes, trying to make it look as though she was just adjusting her hair.

"I couldn't, there was Mark to consider. I had no money, no job, no family to turn to. They'd warned me about Jed before I married him, but I was young, I didn't listen. When I found out they were right, it was too late. I couldn't let them see what he did to me and anyway, they were getting old. Who knows what he would have done to them if I'd gone back home? I was stuck."

"Didn't the hospital report it?"

BM shook her head. "I didn't go. I couldn't admit to anyone that my husband would do such a thing to me. I just stayed put and took painkillers. I wore makeup to cover the bruises on my face and jeans and long sleeved tops to cover the rest of me. About a week later I felt one of you kick." She looked at me, her eyes still wet. "You couldn't imagine the joy I felt. It was like the greatest gift in the world to know you were alive. I didn't know there were two of you, back then, I just knew that my baby had survived."

I watched her, fascinated. This was like some book, not real life. Not my life, my history. I couldn't believe she was telling me all this but it was like she'd held it all in for so long that now it'd found an escape it was gushing out like water from a burst pipe.

"I didn't say anything to Jed. I carried on covering up the best I could. He must have noticed but he didn't do or say anything. I thought, maybe he'd come around to the idea. Whether he had or not I didn't know but I didn't want to break the spell by saying something. While ever he wasn't hitting me, yelling or threatening, I kept my mouth shut and my head down. The next few months I did everything he wanted of me and faster than he could ever want. Some days my back was breaking and the weariness pulled me down like a weight, but I never said anything. I was determined not to upset him. I started in labour when he was out at the pub one night. I went round to my neighbour, Millie. She'd had three kids of her own so knew what she was doing. She knew what Jed was like and didn't question my not wanting to go into hospital. Fortunately because it was my second child the labour was quick. Just six hours. Jed came home in the middle of it so Millie had to break off seeing to me and warm his dinner." BM sighed. "I was so scared when she left me but I didn't dare say anything. I couldn't even cry out, I just bit my lip and panted.

"The first one, you, was born at 11:15 pm on 15th April.

"How do you know which one I am?"

BM smiled, apologetically. "I read all the papers at the time. I knew the nurse called you Rachel, I'm just surprised your adoptive parents didn't change it."

I shrugged, I'd never even thought about that, I mean, I was Rachel and that was it.

"Despite being a twin you were solid, sturdy. You came out screaming." BM continued. She smiled, her eyes distant, like she was seeing it all again. "Such a cute baby, you already had some hair. I took one look at you and fell in love. I knew straight away that I would call you Millie after my neighbour because she was so good to me."

Millie. I was supposed to be Millie. The name seemed strange, foreign, it wasn't me and yet it was; it was who I was meant to be. I felt split, like I was two people all of a sudden. Part of me was still Rachel Brooks teenager but another part was Millie, a tiny baby with a terrified mother and a violent father. I shuddered. What would my life have been like if she hadn't given me up? I started to drift, to wonder, but BM's voice pulled my attention back to her.

"I thought that was it, but the contractions began again. I didn't know what was happening but Millie just urged me to push. Ten minutes later my second little girl arrived with a weak little wail. She was tiny, not strong at all. Straight away I decided to call her Minnie, like Minnie mouse, she was so small. Millie told me you should both be in hospital, me too, but I couldn't, Jed would go crazy. If I wanted to keep you both there had to be no interruption to Jed's routine. Millie cleaned me up and did what was necessary for the two of you. She stayed as long as she could, did some jobs in the house to keep Jed happy and then went back to her own children. She'd left them in the care of the eldest who was only twelve."

"Marcy, are you ready to go back?"

I jumped, I'd been so absorbed I'd never even noticed the tall health care assistant arrive. BM looked just as shocked.

"Oh, Sheila, erm, yes. I'll be with you in a minute. I'm sorry, Rachel, I have to go back to work now but I finish at eight. We could go to my place and talk, if you want." Her eyes pleaded with me to say 'yes'.

Every sensible bone in my body screamed at me to say 'no', but my mouth didn't listen and I found myself saying 'yes'.

My heart jerked with fear as soon as the word left my mouth, like, what was I doing? I didn't even know this woman! But BM beamed, her grin so wide she'd give the Cheshire Cat a run for his money.

"That's great. I'll meet you outside the North Entrance at 8 o'clock then. We'll go to my place, it isn't far and I'll tell you everything you want to know."

Her fingers flitted around each other, like her whole body wanted to dance, but only her fingers dared.

I nodded.

"Okay."

Her eyes softened, "Thank you, Rachel. You don't know how much this means to me."

I nodded sharply then jumped up, almost knocking the chair over. Suddenly I'd got to get out of there. She was like, 'you don't know how much this means to me'. I wasn't doing this for her, I was doing it for me. She dumped me, I needed to know why, so maybe I could feel better about myself. I mean, what did it matter how she felt? She's the one who did the dumping, not me. So she had a violent husband, other women do too but they don't dump their kids.

I marched out of the café and down the corridor, glad that her footsteps didn't follow me. Once outside I took great gulps of air.

"You must be crazy, Rachel, you've gotta be absolutely mental," I muttered to myself as I headed towards Scalby Road. Agreeing to meet her later was probably the most stupid thing I'd ever done but I knew I was still gonna do it. I just had to know why she'd thrown me away. My heart beat so loudly. I'd got a violent birth dad who beat my birth mum and wanted to abort me. I'd even got an older brother. Suddenly I wished I'd asked about him, what he was like, whether she'd given him up as well. It must have been hard on him seeing all that happened between his parents.

I thought about those tiny babies, strong Millie and tiny, Minnie. They sounded like cartoon characters, not real at all and definitely not me.

My breath came in short gasps and my eyes stung. I was gonna cry again, I knew it and there was nothing I could do to stop it. I fished out a tissue and covered my face the best I could. There weren't many people walking to and from the hospital but I didn't want them to know I was crying. I pretended to blow my nose feeling like my heart was being ripped out of my chest. It was like I was back there, a tiny baby, wrapped in a little pink blanket, left alone in a doorway of Doncaster Royal Infirmary. She was the one who'd left me. She'd kept Rebecca and thrown me away. I know she did the same to Rebecca a year later, but what did I do to be first? Was I so awful? I mean, how bad could I be, I was just born? And if her husband was that bad why didn't she abandon us at the same time? At least we could have grown up together.

My hands balled into fists, pressing the tissue against my face. I wanted to scream, shout, thump anything in sight, but I couldn't, if I did they'd have me on the psych ward faster than a downhill skier on wii.

So instead I bit into my fists through the tissue and cried until my head hurt.

A few people walked past giving me funny looks then one old dear stopped and put her wrinkled face next to mine.

"Are you all right, love?" she asked, her voice all soft and caring. "Do you need any help?"

I shook my head.

"I'm okay," I lied.

The old dear nodded and walked on, probably figuring somebody just died or something.

By the time I'd stopped crying and my breathing had returned from short gasps to almost normal, my face was a total wreck. I'd blown my nose so many times there was a red 'wing' up either side of it.

I called for a taxi, unable to face a bus full of people and fixed my face using my little mirror and a mega layer of foundation while I waited. I couldn't do anything about the blood shot eyes. I'd just have to hope nobody looked too closely.

Somehow I'd got to get myself right before going back to meet her later, but I'd already decided, this time I wouldn't be going alone.

CHAPTER THIRTEEN

The taxi turned onto Wykeham Street and I saw him, Joshua, out on the loose, laughing and joking with his mates. A girl in a short skirt walked past them, she looked familiar, I think from a year below me in school. I couldn't hear what they were saying but I knew by their actions, they all turned towards her, their hands making rude gestures. One of them grabbed her arm but she pulled it away and walked off real quick. The gang all laughed like it was this huge joke.

My stomach tightened. Why couldn't they have kept him locked up? That's where he belonged, not out on the streets able to hurt somebody else.

The taxi pulled up outside Gran's so there was no time to think about it anymore. I reached over and paid the driver then climbed out. The gate was open, so I walked straight through and opened the front door.

"So you see, I need to find somewhere quickly before my granddaughter returns to her family." Gran's voice was shaky and coming from the sitting room.

"Well the process can take some time, Mrs Banks, however, given the circumstances I think we could find you a place more quickly."

I frowned at the woman's words and walked quickly into the sitting room.

"Find a place where, Gran?" I asked.

Gran's head shot up towards me like a bomb'd exploded or something.

"Rachel, I never heard you come in," she said, her cheeks flushing pink.

"I just arrived," I said, lamely. "A place where Gran?"

The short haired woman on the settee, turned towards me. She held a clip board in her hand with what looked like a form she'd filled in. A leather brief case leaned against the settee next to her leg.

"Oh, hello," she said, all smiles, "You must be Rachel, or is it Rebecca?"

"Rachel," I said, my voice dull.

"Well, my name is Mandy Weathers and I'm from Social Services. We are going to find your Grandma a nice place in an aged person's care home so she can be well looked after when you return home."

I felt like I'd just been thumped in the stomach. My mouth gaped open like a baby bird and I stared at the woman, then at Gran.

"An old folk's home? Gran?"

Gran, half grimaced, half smiled.

"I have no choice, Rachel. You know how I've been. It's not safe for an old woman like me out on the streets anymore. At least in a nice home I will be well looked after and will have other people to talk to."

"You really want this?" I asked, my voice almost a whisper.

The nod of Gran's head was hardly visible. Her lips pursed.

"It's the best thing, Rachel."

Then I knew, it wasn't the best thing, it wasn't even what Gran wanted. She was just scared. Until that slime Joshua attacked her, she'd never said anything about going into a home. She'd been happy with her independence, in fact she'd loved it. She'd always said she'd never be found dead in 'one of those places' and here she was planning to go in.

"I've already given the place a good clean for the next person but I'll need you to help me pack before you go. I cannot do it on my own, especially with this."

She held out her injured wrist.

So that's what all the manic cleaning was about. I couldn't say anything. There was a whole load of things I wanted to say, but my throat wouldn't work and anyway, I knew it'd do no good. There was only one thing that'd work and that was having Joshua Green locked up so Gran'd feel safe again. So I just nodded, bit my lip and feeling the tears coming again I backed out of the room and into my bedroom.

I pulled out my mobile, my chest tight like somebody was standing on it.

"Where r u?" I texted Rebecca.

My phone beeped.

"Ur Gran sent us out. Me & L been in town. Met up wi ur mates. L gone back to B&B now."

"Cum ome now!" I texted back.

"KK wots up?"

"Just cum." I texted back.

I heard the front door open and close. The social worker had gone, but Gran didn't come into my room. I guess she figured it was safer to avoid me for a while. I just sat on my bed rocking and biting my nails. I couldn't believe all this was happening at once. The birth mother thing, Gran's mugging and now this! My brain went into overdrive trying to come up with answers and by the time Rebecca walked through the door, I knew exactly what I had to do. She sat down beside me on my bed and wrapped her arm around my shoulders.

"Was it her, the birth mother? What did she do?" Rebecca looked like she had something sour in her mouth.

141

"Her name's Marcy."

"Oh."

"That's what the health care assistant called her."

Rebecca didn't say anything.

"She said we've got an older brother."

Rebecca grunted. "Did she abandon him as well?"

"I don't know, she didn't say." I took a deep breath. "Our birth father was violent, he used to beat her."

Rebecca's eyes narrowed. "Are we supposed to feel sorry for her now?"

I shrugged.

"I don't know the whole story. I'm gonna see her later. We're gonna talk some more."

"You're gonna meet her later?"

"Yeah."

"I'm coming."

"You want to see her?"

"No, I want to make sure you're okay."

I shook my head.

"No, I thought maybe Luke'd come with me seeing as you're not exactly, well, you know, you don't like her."

"That's an understatement," Rebecca said, frowning. "So if birth mother's not the one who upset you, who is?"

"It's Gran," I said, "When I came home she was talking to a social worker about going into a home." Even saying it was hard.

"So that's why she got rid of us," Rebecca said. "Bet she wasn't happy about you walking in on them then."

"No, she looked a bit shocked. But, don't you see? It's Joshua Green. While ever he's out there,

142

Gran's not gonna feel safe. I saw him on my way home in the taxi, laughing and joking with his mates, like everything's okay. He's outside and Gran's locked up in here. If she goes into an old folk's home she'll never come out. She'll never be my old Gran again. You know?"

Rebecca nodded.

"So, what are you going to do?"

I rubbed my palms against my forehead.

"My head hurts, there's just too much to think about." I sighed. "But I think I've come up with something."

As I explained Rebecca's eyes gleamed. When I'd finished she grinned.

"Fantastic! It's exactly what that mongrel deserves."

"So, you're with me?"

"Yeah, if you can round up enough others."

I bit my lip. "I should be able to. There's Sam, Ruby, Sapphire and Summer. Then there's me, you and Luke. I reckon Sam and the others will be able to round up a few more..." My insides did a sort of, jelly wobble. "Do you really think it's the right thing to do? I mean, it's not the sort of thing I'd normally do and you know what happened before."

"'Course it's the right thing!" Rebecca's eyes shone, "Look, I know it's not what you'd normally do, but sometimes you've got no choice. Once we're through with him, he'll be begging to confess. Anyway, it's for your gran don't forget. Unless we do summat she'll never get her life back."

She'd said the right thing. Thinking of Gran all bent and curled up in a high seat chair made up my mind. I straightened my back, my head high, determined now.

143

"I'll tell Luke on the way back from Marcy's, you know, the birth mother's."

"Umph."

I reckon I'd got no doubt what Rebecca thought of that!

I texted Luke and he agreed to go with me to Marcy's. He was all for it, thought it was a great idea so long as I wasn't going alone.

Gran made tea. She was real quiet. Rebecca kept a monologue going as neither Gran or me were up to saying anything. It was only a couple of hours before I had to go meet BM and with that and my mind spinning with plots against Joshua, I just wanted to spew. I nearly choked on my tea and spent the last hour in the bathroom. Gran even offered me some Diacalm.

She stood in the hallway, pale and somehow smaller than normal as I pulled on my jacket.

"Rachel, Love, are you sure you should be going out with ..." she nodded towards my rear end. "You know."

"Graaaan!" I felt my face burn and could see Rebecca standing behind her a grin stretched so wide it nearly touched her hair at both sides.

"Well," Gran went on, "It would not do to want to 'you know' while walking out with your boyfriend, now would it? It could be quite a turn off."

"Graannn!" I couldn't believe this.

Rebecca had clamped her lips together and her shoulders were shaking. I glared at her.

"I'll be all right," I said as firmly as I could manage. "See you later, Gran."

"Bye, Love. But you take care. You have to be kind to your bowels, you know."

A snort erupted from Rebecca and she clamped her hand over her mouth.

"It's no laughing matter, young lady," said Gran, rounding on Rebecca and sounding a bit more like her old self. "Bowels are important."

Rebecca nodded and muttered, "I know," through her fingers, but I could tell she was trying really hard not to snort again.

I narrowed my eyes at her.

"I'll see *you* later as well," I muttered then turned and got out of there quickly before the conversation went down hill any further.

Luke was waiting for me.

"What's with the red face?" he asked, his own bruises still a mess.

I quickly told him and had to put up with his jokes all the way to the hospital.

"Tell me if you get *caught short*," he said, as we sat near the back of an almost empty bus. "You can always talk to me if you're *desperate* for help. I'm here at your *convenience*. We could even collar a *PC* if you feel *the urge*, I'm sure they'll lend a hat off their *head*."

"All right, all right." I shot him a 'shut up or else' look. "We're nearly there so quit, okay?"

"Okay, I'll *can* it. You're looking a bit *flush* anyway."

"Luke!" I hissed.

"All right," he said and held up his arms in mock surrender. "It got you here without you working yourself up into a massive panic fit though, didn't it?"

That shut me up. He was right, we were here at the hospital and I felt okay. Or at least I did until I looked out of the window and saw her. She was standing at the bus stop, still wearing her uniform with the same blue cardigan pulled around her shoulders. My stomach suddenly did a triple somersault. This was it. I was gonna find out about my past but now it came to it, I wasn't really sure I wanted to know. I mean, what if it was all bad news? It hadn't been very good so far.

Marcy half smiled as I stepped down off the bus and glanced over my shoulder at Luke.

"I live not far from here," she said, her fingers squirming like worms in a bucket.

I just nodded and followed. Luke stayed a couple of steps behind me like a mark of respect or something.

We walked out of the hospital grounds, turned towards the crematorium, then onto Hovingham Drive. I was too nervous to notice which of the connecting avenues we turned onto, but was surprised to see a nice row of semi-detached houses. Marcy's was about half way along. It had a small lawn in front, cut and trimmed neatly. Her doors and windows were white framed and double glazed with blue curtains. She unlocked the door, then turned, her head slightly bowed.

"Both my parents died last year, they left me some money. I bought this house a couple of months ago. It was a fresh start for me." She was almost apologetic like I'd think she'd got no right to it or something.

"Oh," I said, not sure what else to say. I wasn't really interested in the house. I was here for one reason only and then I wanted to get out. She shuffled a bit, like she was expecting more, but when I didn't say anything else, she opened the door and stepped in. I followed but Luke stayed outside.

"Isn't your young man coming in?" She asked when I'd followed her through to the kitchen. The walls were painted pale yellow, the cupboards a deeper yellow. Even the work surfaces looked yellow but maybe they were just reflecting off the cupboards and walls. It was like standing inside the sun. Realising I was just gazing around like an idiot, I managed to focus and answer her.

"No, he's waiting outside."

She smiled, I think she was happy it was just the two of us.

"Would you like a drink?"

I nodded, holding a drink in my hands would give them something to do. Right now they were jammed in my jacket pockets, playing with the dust or lint or whatever it is that gathers in the corner.

"Tea?"

I nodded. "Yes, thanks."

Like Rebecca, I didn't really like tea but I was struggling to talk so it was easier just to let her get on with it.

"Please, sit down."

She looked at the wooden kitchen chair on my side of the small wooden table. I pulled out the chair and cringed as it scraped across the yellow lino. I sat down without pulling it back in to stop it scraping again. I watched her back as she filled the kettle then reached up to the cupboards and retrieved two mugs followed by a tub with tea bags.

"What's your full name?" I asked, as the kettle boiled and she poured steaming water into each mug.

"Marcy Emily Phelps." She clattered a spoon around the mugs and put them on the table. She slid one across to me, followed by a yellow bowl. "Sugar?"

I shook my head. "No thanks."

"Sounds fancy doesn't it? Marcy Phelps. Should belong to some high faluting person, not me." She wrapped both hands around her mug as I had done.

I guess she needed as much comfort as me. She sighed. "My life's been far from fancy."

I waited for her to go on but she just sat there, staring into her mug. I chewed my lip wondering whether she was waiting for me to say something, but I didn't know what I was supposed to say.

In the end the question that burned in my heart forced its way out.

"Why did you abandon us?" I whispered.

Marcy flinched as though I'd hit her. She swallowed hard and gripped her mug like her life depended on it. She was quiet for so long, I thought she'd never say another word, but then she looked up.

"You deserve to know the truth but it won't be easy to hear. Are you sure you want me to tell you?"

Pressing my lips together I nodded. It was like a vile craving. I didn't want to know but a part of me couldn't survive without hearing every detail.

Marcy paused for a minute. The only sound was the ticking of the clock high on the wall.

"I told you about your birth earlier, didn't I?"

I nodded, I'd got a strange mixture of longing, excitement and fear all packed into my chest. It was so tight I felt like I was suffocating, there was no chance of me saying a word.

Marcy swallowed then sat up straighter like she found some strength or determination from somewhere.

"All right." She sighed. "Well, after I'd given birth I was back up and working within hours. I wanted you both so much, I couldn't let Jed have any reason to get rid of you. He didn't acknowledge either of you, it was as though you weren't there. The whole atmosphere in the house was charged. I didn't dare speak and tried to keep the both of you quiet. At the first squeak I was there feeding or holding you, just enough to quiet you down then back to work. It was okay for a few days, but then both of you started to cry more. I couldn't understand it Jed began murmuring, then shouting at me to shut you both up. I was frantic, I couldn't understand what was setting you off, but when one started the other did as well." She looked up at me, her knuckles white against her mug.

"I did my best, honestly I did. Jed couldn't stand the crying. I'd quieten you down but as soon as I left you, one or the other would set off again. I wanted to take you to the doctor's but I couldn't because they didn't know about you, I hadn't even registered you yet. It was stupid really but back then I was so afraid. It was like I had to keep pretending nothing had changed so Jed would let me keep you." She shook her head. "It was irrational really."

"When you were nearly two weeks old Jed snapped. You'd both been crying none stop. Jed had shouted, even hit me a couple of times and in the end he jumped out of his chair and headed for the stairs. His face was red with hate and anger. I was sure he'd kill you both. I dove in front of him, promising I'd quieten you. He just grabbed me and flung me out of his way. I crashed back into the wall, my head hitting the banister rail with a sickening thud. Pain shot through my skull and tears filled my eyes. I was half blinded by them, but I couldn't let him hurt you. I pulled myself up and raced up stairs after him. They were really narrow and steep so I couldn't get past him. I just followed behind, begging and pleading for him to leave you alone." Marcy's face was pale, her eyes wide with fear, like she was living it all over again.

"He reached the bedroom and headed for the cot. It was Mark's old cot, painted blue. You were both lying there, your little arms and legs waving around, escaping from beneath your pink blankets. Your little faces red and tear streaked. Jed marched right up to the cot and grabbed you, Rachel. He dragged you out, holding you upside down by one leg, your little body dangling. You screamed even louder."

My heart raced inside my chest, I couldn't believe I was that little baby.

"'Get rid of them or I will'," he said. I couldn't breathe, convinced he'd drop you. 'Please, Jed,' I pleaded. 'Let me keep them.' 'No,' he roared. He was waving you about like a rag. I tried to think fast and said the first thing I could think of, a compromise. 'Let me keep one of them, please.' I begged. He stood there, weighing it up. You were still dangling there, your little face turning deep red with all the blood rushing to your head. 'Get rid of one,' he said, then swung you at me. I managed to catch you, but I was gasping for breath. My chest constricted and blood roared in my ears. I'd been so sure he would drop you. So sure. I knew I had no choice, one of you had to go to save you both."

I watched her, the corners of my eyes wet. I couldn't believe that was my history, the past I'd wanted to discover.

"Why me?" I managed to whisper, my bottom lip trembling. I was like, really biting down hard on it, but it still wobbled. Any minute now I was gonna lose the fight and burst into tears. I could feel my hands shaking around the mug, tea splashing around inside. I released my grip and pushed my hands down under the table and into my lap where she couldn't see them. "Why did you get rid of me? Was I the worst?"

Marcy shook her head. "No! I didn't want to lose either of you, but when it came to a choice, it had to be you. You see Minnie, Rebecca, was so tiny, you

150

were so much stronger. It was safer to leave you somewhere."

"Why didn't you just go to Social Services? Why just dump me?" My voice caught in my throat and the tears escaped. "Didn't you care what happened to me?"

My heart was pounding real loud now, it's a wonder she couldn't hear it. My head pounded along with it, right in the middle above my eyes. It was like somebody was sitting in there, hitting my scull from the inside.

Marcy looked at me, her eyes reaching out like they were trying to get right inside me.

"Of course I cared, but I was scared. I knew Jed wouldn't want officials coming to the house or being involved. There were so many marks on you two, they might have taken all three of you away," she gasped and stopped, like she'd said more than she should.

"He abused us?" I said, my voice cracking.

Marcy shook her head. "I don't know, they weren't bad marks just little red patches. I wasn't sure. I wanted to ask my friend Millie but even she might have reported us if she thought he was hurting you. I couldn't bare the thought of losing you all."

"So why didn't you get rid of us both at the same time, to keep us safe?" I demanded.

A sob escaped Marcy's throat, her eyes wet. "I couldn't bare it. I was selfish I suppose. I didn't want to lose either of you, you were my little girls. But I knew one had to go and I really thought that once there was only one of you it would be okay. I thought Millie would be safe. It broke my heart to wrap you up in your little blanket and take you to the hospital. I left you on the doorstep where I knew you'd be found then hid behind a wall to watch. It only took ten minutes before someone came out. It was a nurse, she looked shocked, then picked you up real gently. She cradled you and rocked you, then searched around. I wanted to run and grab you away from her but I knew that if I loved you I had to let you go so you could have a better life. I cried all the way home. For months I watched the news and read all the papers to see how you were. I can't tell you how hard it was. I felt like a huge piece of me had been broken off and would never be repaired. I focused all my attention on Minnie and Mark. I made sure I did everything for Jed so he'd let me keep Minnie. She cried for a few days, I think she knew you'd gone. Jed started to get mad again, but then one day she just stopped.

"Things were better without me?" It was weird. Hearing about this family there was no way I wanted to be part of it, but at the same time I wanted them to miss me.

"Things were quieter but not better. How could they be better without my child?" Marcy looked into my eyes, like she was trying to transfer all her emotion into me. I looked away, I didn't want it.

"I'm sorry, Rachel." She shook her head. "I'm sorry I let you down. Maybe I could have fought harder to keep you. I should have."

"What happened with Rebecca?" My voice was flat, I didn't want her apologies, I just wanted the facts so I could get out of there.

Marcy sighed. "As I said, it was quiet for a while, but Jed started drinking more heavily. He regularly came home drunk and always found something wrong. It could be something tiny like a shirt not ironed as he wanted it or the wrong meat on his dinner. It didn't matter really it was just an excuse to start on me." Her head hung so low I couldn't see her face at all.

"One night, as he was shouting at me, Minnie started to cry. He screamed for me to shut her up. I tried, but his continued shouting just upset her more. He hit me while she was in my arms. I fell and just managed to save her from the impact by wrapping my arms around her. I fell so heavily all the wind was knocked out of me. Minnie screamed at the top of her little lungs. Jed grabbed her up by the legs, just as he'd done to you. She dangled there in his big hands, her arms flailing."

"'I'll teach her to scream!' He yelled, swinging her in his hand. It was like all his hate and rage was focused on her."

"I was convinced he was going to throw her across the room. I pulled myself up, holding out my arms, begging him to give her to me. He swung her about for longer, taunting me, then he threw her at me and barked, 'Keep her quiet!' as I caught her. That was when I knew, I had to get her out of the house too to save her. I'd still never registered her, I'd been terrified they'd ask questions, figure out about you and take all my kids. I'd read you'd been adopted. I wanted you to be together so I wrapped her in her pink blanket, identical to yours and left her on the exact spot. I even left a note explaining that you were twins and asking that you be placed together. As I watched a gust of wind whipped up the note and blew it away over a nearby wall. Before I could retrieve it a nurse came out and found Minnie. I didn't know what to do. I so desperately wanted you to grow up together. When they realised the similar circumstances and DNA testing proved you were twins, I was so happy, at least you would have each other ..." She shook her head again. "I never imagined you'd end up apart."

Before I could say anything the front door crashed open. Both of us jumped and a look of panic crossed Marcy's face. I sat rigid like a statue hearing footsteps coming down the hall and wishing I was anywhere but there.

CHAPTER FOURTEEN

I felt each step vibrate in my bones as they approached the kitchen. My heart pounded in rhythm until they reached the doorway and stomped in. I twisted around, my chest so tight it felt like a thousand rubber bands were strapped around it. I expected to see a huge, mean, middle-aged man but instead I looked up into the spotty fat face of a boy. He looked about eighteen with lines between his eyes so deep it looked like he'd been frowning since birth.

His blue eyes fixed on mine and shot hate missiles at me.

"What's *she* doing here?" He demanded, like I was a hair in his dinner or something.

Marcy stood, her hands shaking.

"Oh, Mark, this is Rachel. Erm, she's your sister, Millie."

"She's not my sister. I haven't got any sisters," he spat.

"Yes, you have," Marcy said, her voice weak. "Remember, I told you…"

"I don't remember. Get rid of her. Where's my dinner?" Mark marched around the kitchen towards the oven. He wasn't exactly fat he was more, like, solid. Nothing wobbled on him, he was just huge. He opened the oven door and bent nearly double to look inside. He looked like he belonged in a strong man competition or something.

"You haven't even got dinner on!" He stormed, turning towards Marcy, who backed away.

She'd turned into a quivering wreck and physically shrunk, her head ducked down into her shoulders like she was trying to disappear.

"I was talking to Rachel. I'll get on with it now," she groveled.

I stared at her unable to believe she could be this frightened of her own son. I stood, the chair scraping across the floor.

"It's all right, I'll go now, let you get on." I was already backing to the door. Marcy followed me.

"I'm sorry," she whispered. "He has a temper like his dad. He wasn't always like this, he started to change after his dad went to prison."

"Prison?"

Marcy nodded, gently pushing me down the hall. "I began to stand up to him after you both ... left. He didn't like it, he hit me more and more but somehow I didn't care any more. It went on for a few years, getting worse until it got so bad our neighbour, Millie called the police. Jed was arrested. I was in hospital for about six weeks. Poor Mark was put in care until I got out. I don't think he's ever forgiven me for that. I decided I'd had enough and pressed charges, for Mark's sake as well as mine. Jed's been inside for eight years now."

"I'm sorry," I said. I wasn't sure what else I could say.

"It's okay," Marcy said, touching my arm. "You take care now. Maybe we could talk again before you go back?"

"Mum!" Mark's voice barked out from the kitchen.

I shrugged. "Maybe."

I didn't know whether I wanted to see her again or not. I know I didn't want to come to this house.

There was no way I wanted to see Mark again, that was one brother I did not want or miss.

Marcy nodded.

"Bye then," she said and quickly shut the door behind me.

As I walked out onto the pavement I could hear Mark's deep angry voice yelling. I couldn't tell what he was saying but I felt sorry for Marcy but at the same time angry with her. He was her son, she should've taught him respect years ago. My dad was always banging on about teaching respect from childhood and it'd last a lifetime. Guilt prodded my stomach, it was easy for me to say but Marcy had been put down for years. It was probably hard to stand firm, when somebody had always treated her like she was nothing.

I shuddered. I was gonna make sure whoever I married was no way like that. First sign of trouble and I'd be out of there. Luke was okay, it'd be good if it was Luke.

"How'd it go?" Luke was waiting a couple of doors down, leaning back against a low garden wall. "Who's the bull?"

I grimaced. "That was my older brother, Mark."

Luke's eyes widened. "Yeah?" He grinned. "I'm glad you don't look like him."

I grinned back. "Yeah, me too."

I filled him in on what Marcy had told me as we walked. He just kept shaking his head and saying 'Wow.' It was kind of hard for us to imagine what her life must've been like and what it was still like with Mark at home.

Finally I told him my plans for Joshua.

"No way, Rachel. You can't do that!" He stopped walking and grabbed my arm.

157

I was like, totally stunned. "Why can't I? I thought you'd go along with it. I mean, we've got to do it for Gran."

Luke shook his head. "Look, I know you want to help your gran but ganging up on Joshua is crazy!"

"It's what he'd do." I folded my arms, my chest hurting. Why was Luke being like this?

"Exactly," Luke said, "It is what Joshua would do and we're better than him."

"Look," I said, my hands on my hips now, reminding me of Rebecca. "All we do is threaten him, yeah? If there's enough of us who tell him we're gonna kick his head in unless he goes to the police and confesses, he'll do it. We won't really have to hurt him, he'll see we're serious and go turn himself in."

"Don't be stupid, Rach. There's no way he's going to walk into the police station and confess just because you and some friends threaten him. He's more likely to say that if you touch him he'll come after your gran and really hurt her."

My stomach tightened, I hadn't thought of that. But then I shook my head. "If he makes any threats like that then we'll show him what'll happen to *him* if anything happens to Gran. We can hurt him a bit and say it'll be worse if he ever goes anywhere near her again."

Luke shook his head again, blowing out air like he was completely emptying his lungs.

"Just listen to yourself. You just don't get it, do you? If you don't beat him up he'll not do anything and he might even come after your gran again. If you do beat him up then you're no better than him and you could end up getting locked up yourself."

"Well, what am I supposed to do?" I yelled. "Just sit back and let him get away with it? He's out

158

there laughing and joking with his mates while Gran's putting herself in a home for the rest of her life! I've got less than two weeks to get this sorted and he's not gonna confess without a push."

We'd reached a busy street and people were staring at us as they walked past. Some of them stepped around us, leaning away like they thought we'd fling out our arms and smack them or something. But then, I was kind of waving my arms around so I couldn't blame them, but I couldn't help it, Luke was making me so mad. I kind of saw his point, but he didn't see mine at all. He was supposed to be my boyfriend, support and help me, but he was the only one who wasn't helping. I'd already texted Sam and the others and they were all in. They all thought it was a good idea. I reckon they'd all had enough of Joshua over the years and figured it was about time they got their own back.

"Rachel, think about it." Luke sounded like he was trying to explain something to a three-year-old. "We've already been picked up by the police, I could've been locked up then, I'm on my last warning, don't forget."

"Oh, so it's all about you then, is it?" I jumped in. "You want to keep yourself safe and you don't care about me and Gran. Some boyfriend you turned out to be!"

"Rachel, I'm not saying that!" Luke ran his hands through his blond hair, a move that normally made my knees weak, but not today, I was too angry. After all I'd been through that afternoon with Marcy and the brother from the Black Lagoon, I needed support not arguments.

"So what are you saying?"

Luke sighed. "I'm saying that the police already have your name too, we could all get locked up and what good would that do your gran? There's got to be a better way."

"Okay, so what is it? I'm listening." I folded my arms, my back stiff and straight.

Luke shrugged. "I don't know, but I'm sure there's a way if we think about it."

I huffed. "Well you go back to your B&B and think about it. We'll have it all sorted and be back home before you come up with anything."

I turned to go, but Luke caught my arm again.

"Rachel?" His eyes were soft, sort of pleading with me. I nearly melted but managed to look away in time. I pulled my arm free and snapped back.

"Just go, Luke. Go back to Rotherham. You always leave me when I need you most!"

I knew that wasn't fair, I was being really mean, but I couldn't stop myself. When I was searching for Rebecca, Luke sometimes didn't agree with me, making me feel like he was letting me down. It wasn't true, but that's how I felt and I felt the same way now.

Luke gasped, his face screwed up like I'd stuck a knife in him.

He didn't say anything. He just stood there shaking his head, then took a couple of steps away. He turned, looking back over his shoulder.

"I can't believe you said that," he said. "Sometimes I don't know you, Rachel and it's obvious you don't know me. I'll be at the B&B," he looked down at the pavement. "I'll stay until tomorrow lunch time. If you want me, you know where I am. If I don't hear from you by then I'll go."

"Don't bother waiting," I said, my mouth dry. "I've got all the help I need."

I turned away from him, my heart hurting. I clenched my hands into fists so tight my fingers ached. I needed him so much right now I needed him to tell me I was doing the right thing. As I marched away my mind was all over the place. Was Luke right? Should we do this? It wasn't something I'd normally do, but I didn't know what else to try. I'd got to stop Joshua for Gran's sake, she needed my help. More than anything I wanted my mum, my real mum, Janet. She'd been there all my life and always had answers for everything. She'd know what to do, she'd sort it but Gran said I couldn't contact her. Biting my lip, I sighed.

'Oh Gran. Why did you have to stop me ringing Mum? I can't do this on my own.'

I walked and walked, part of me knowing Luke was right and the other part pushing the thought away. I was only doing what had to be done, that's all. If there was another way, I'd take it.

It was dark when I finally got back to Gran's and Rebecca pounced on me as soon as I walked in.

"Where've you been?" she hissed, looking over her shoulder down the hall to make sure Gran was nowhere near.

"I needed to walk," I said taking off my jacket and hanging it up on one of the pegs on my right.

"And you've never heard of the phone?"

"Take a chill pill, Rebecca, you sound like my mother." I pushed passed her into the sitting room.

"Oh, that's great, that is. I stay here and look after *your* gran all night, covering for you when she wonders where you are for so long and you tell me to chill? I was worried sick about you, I mean, you were going to see the physco stalker. Anything could've happened and what thanks do I get? *'You sound like my mother.*'" She finished in a mocking voice. "Nice to be appreciated."

"Look, I'm sorry, okay?" I slumped into the rocking chair and sat looking down at my hands. "It's been a rotten day, okay? I just needed some time. I should've rung, I just didn't think about it. I forgot I turned my phone off when I went to see her."

Rebecca sank onto the settee opposite.

"Was it that bad?" she asked, her voice softer.

I shrugged. "She told me all about her life. Her husband battered her, threatened to do the same to us, that's why she gave us away."

"She didn't give us away, she dumped us." Bitterness oosed from Rebecca.

"Whatever." I didn't have the energy to argue. "We've got this rotten brother called Mark, he's about eighteen. Looked at me like I was a piece of dirt when he walked in. But that wasn't the worst."

Rebecca sat and waited.

"Luke thinks going after Joshua's a bad idea. He was like, real mean about it. He said I was as bad as Joshua and unless I come crawling back to him by tomorrow dinner time, he's going home to Rotherham."

Rebecca listened, then shrugged.

"His loss."

"Rebecca! I love him." I'd said it without thinking and sat there, sort of stunned. Yes, I did, I did love him.

"So ring him, tell him he's right."

"But he's not right."

"So ring him and tell him he's wrong."

"I already told him that." I sighed. "Oh, I don't know, I'll figure something out. Look, is everybody okay to go look for Joshua tomorrow?"

"I've not had any texts, so nobody's changed their mind, unless you've had one."

I pulled my phone out of my bag and switched it on, listening for the familiar beep that'd tell me I'd got a text, but there was silence. I checked the settings, made sure the sound was on. I even checked the inbox, but there was nothing.

I couldn't stop the tears.

"Rachel?" Rebecca slid off the settee and knelt beside me.

"He hasn't texted," I whimpered, "I thought he'd have texted."

"Give him time, by tomorrow he'll figure out you're right. Then he'll probably text and ask to come with us."

I wanted that so much, but I shook my head.

"He won't. It's over. He's going home tomorrow."

"Well, why don't we go get Joshua early? Then you can go to the B & B, tell him it worked and everything'll be okay again."

Every part of my heart and body ached, hoping she was right. I swiped the tears away with the back of my hand and nodded. I couldn't speak, too big a part of me said that was never gonna happen. Luke and me were finished. Joshua was gonna get away with everything. Gran would go into an old person's home forever and there was nothing I could do about any of it.

CHAPTER FIFTEEN

The next day we had breakfast early then left Gran watching her favourite morning TV and headed off to meet the others outside Sainsbury's.

My stomach had done so many back flips all morning my breakfast had been half a slice of toast, chucked up in the bathroom five minutes later. Thankfully the cool morning air started to revive me a bit and I felt almost human by the time we met the others. Sapphire, Ruby, Summer and Sam stood in a little huddle with their boyfriends Jake, Nathan, Brandon and Keiran. Shoppers stared nervously at them as they walked past. I couldn't blame them really, Ruby's boyfriend, Nathan had snake tattoos down his arm and his eyebrows pierced. Summer's boyfriend, Keiran was like, six foot and you couldn't see Jake's face because of his hoody. Jake's jeans were torn and he stood slouched over with his hands in his pockets. They looked a rough bunch but I knew them all and they were all great lads. Only Sapphire's boyfriend, Brandon, looked young and innocent, but he was actually the most mischievous of the lot.

"Thanks for coming," I said, my hands twisting in my jacket pockets.

Keiran grinned. "No trouble, we like a good scrap and Joshua's been asking for it forever."

My stomach felt like Keiran had just reached inside and tied it into a knot.

"We're not gonna hit him," I said quickly, "We're just gonna make him think we are."

164

"That's not what Sam said," Keiran nodded towards my friend who stared innocently down at her trainers. "She told Jake there's no way Joshua's gonna own up to mugging your gran so we're gonna kick his face in."

"Sam!" My hands clenched. "I thought you agreed this'd work? I don't want to hurt him if we can help it and even then, not much."

Sam looked up and met my eyes.

"It will work if we knock his block off. He's not gonna confess just from a threat."

She looked so certain I began to wish I hadn't come up with this. The last thing I wanted was to get violent like Joshua. Maybe Luke was right. Just thinking about him made me want to rush straight off and make up with him.

Rebecca must've seen the confusion in my face because she stepped up beside me.

"Look, I don't know Joshua like you do, but most people like him are basically cowards. If we can get him on his own, without his gang, I reckon he'll soon cave in."

Sam shrugged. "Whatever." But I could see she wasn't convinced. "So let's get this going then, hey? Where are we gonna look first?"

I sighed. "I reckon we split up and search. We can ring each other on our mobiles if we find him."

Everybody nodded.

"But no one does anything until I get there, okay?" I added, quickly.

Sam saluted. "Yes, Boss."

Ruby, Sapphire, Nathan and Brandon set off towards the beach. Sam and Jake headed towards Peasholme Park, their arms wrapped around each other. I doubted any searching would be done once they got

165

among the trees. Rebecca, me, Summer and Keiran stayed around town.

We walked down by the train station and checked the park opposite. Nothing. We checked Brunswick shopping centre and the shops we thought would interest him but there was no sign.

After an hour I rang Sam.

"Er ... yeah?" Sam panted.

"Can you prise your lips away from Jake long enough to talk?" I asked, smiling despite everything.

"Hey! We've been looking!"

"Yeah, sure, over each other's shoulders while you suck tonsils."

I heard Sam snort.

"Sussed. Anyway, we have looked and he's not here. Ruby and Nathan went up to the cemetery and he's not there either."

I bit my lip.

"I've been thinking, it's still early. What if he's still at home?"

I heard what sounded like a slap.

"What's that?" I asked.

"Me hitting my stupid forehead," Sam said, "What an absolute idiot. Of course Joshua's not gonna be up this early, not unless somebody puts a bomb under his bed. He was always late for school and he's not gonna be any different now he's left. Where's my brain?"

"Thinking about Jake's tonsils," I said. Rebecca watched, her head on one side. She shrugged a 'what's going on?'

"Sam, I'll ring for a couple of taxis. You get everybody to text me where they are and we'll pick everybody up."

Our taxi pulled up a few doors away from Joshua's house. It was semi-detached, with paint peeling from the window frames and door. A fence with a couple of slats missing here and there surrounded the front garden. I'd expected the garden to be over grown, I don't know why, I suppose it's what my mum would call prejudice, but it wasn't. The lawn was neat and trimmed and surrounded by a border of bright pink and yellow flowers.

"Pssch!"

The hiss came from our left. I turned and spotted Sapphire's pale face peeping out from behind a garden wall, two houses back. The six of us, we'd picked up Ruby and Nathan on the way, walked over and were pulled down by Sam.

"Get down," she whispered. "Someone keeps looking out of one of the windows. You don't want them to see you, do you?"

I shook my head and looked round. Everyone was here crouched behind the low wall.

I looked up at the house belonging to the garden we were hiding in. The curtains were drawn and all was quiet. I hoped we'd be gone before they woke up because they'd have a fit if they opened their curtains and found their garden crowded with crouching teenagers.

Fortunately, the front door of Joshua's house opened right then and Joshua himself stepped out, his face half hidden by his grey hoody.

"I'm going out," he called back through the door. There must have been a reply because he shrugged and shouted, "Whatever," before slouching out onto the pavement, his hands deep in the pockets of his torn jeans.

"There's a wide alley, just up that way," Sam whispered, watching Joshua head away from us. "If a couple of the lads set off now they could push him in there as he passes. Then the rest of us can join them and get this sorted."

I didn't speak, I couldn't. Now it came to it, I just didn't want to do this anymore.

"Rach!" she hissed.

"Okay," I croaked, there just wasn't time for me to figure this out.

Sam nodded at Jake then he and Nathan stood and set off after Joshua. I clenched my teeth, trying to ignore the nagging feeling that this was very wrong.

CHAPTER SIXTEEN

I peeked out from behind the wall and watched Nathan and Jake closing in on Joshua. They grabbed him from behind. He didn't even have time to struggle before he was pushed roughly into the alley. Sam, me and the others all jumped up and followed.

"Get off me!" I heard him shout as we reached the entrance to the alley.

The alley was about two metres wide and ran the depth of the nearby houses then along the back walls of their gardens. Broken cardboard boxes lay strewn about, obviously somebody around here hadn't heard of recycling. Other than that it was just bare cement floor and high red brick walls bordering the neighbouring houses.

"Take him round the corner," Sam instructed. "There's less chance anyone will see anything then."

The image of Emma ordering her cronies to take me outside the school gates shot into my mind. They'd grabbed me and pushed me around the corner just as Nathan and Jake did to Joshua now. I shut my inner ears to the cry that this was wrong, reminding myself that this had to be done, for Gran. I followed them. The path ran along the length of the row of houses, finishing with a dead end in both directions.

Nathan and Jake let go of Joshua leaving him standing alone in the middle of a semi-circle of frowning faces.

"Oh, it's you," he spat, as soon as he saw me. His stance suddenly changed, instead of crouching, he stood up straight and confident. "Is this about your stupid grandmother again? Or is it about your pathetic boyfriend? Where is he, anyway? Sulking? Licking his wounds? The coward!"

"Shut up, Joshua!" I surprised myself with the authority in my voice. Where did that come from? Was it because he was insulting Luke? Luke was not pathetic and he wasn't licking any wounds, he was way too tough for that, he was just being sensible.

I blinked. If Luke was sensible for staying away then what was I doing here? I shook my head, pushing those thoughts from my mind. He wasn't right, this had to be done, for Gran.

I shot hate daggers from my eyes at Joshua and hoped they were enough to let him know I meant business.

"Look, Joshua. We both know that you mugged my gran so I'm giving you one last chance. Go and confess, or else."

Joshua sneered.

"Or else what?"

"Or else I let these lads beat the stuffing out of you."

"As if! You, soppy little Rachel Brooks is gonna set her little friends onto me? Yeah, tell me another one." His words sounded confident, but I noticed his eyes flitting along the line of my friends. He was scared.

I heard Keiran growl beside me.

"You said yourself that I've changed, Joshua. Do you really want to find out how far I'll go to make sure Gran's safe?" I was bluffing, but I hoped he couldn't tell. I hoped my acting skills were good enough, they'd helped in Rotherham when things got tough.

Joshua smirked. "You haven't changed that much, Brooks." He stepped towards me. "Now get out

170

of my way, the lot of you!" His eyes focused on mine. "Or you'll be the ones regretting it."

He came right up to me and tried to push me out of the way, but before he could Keiran and Jake were on him. His eyes and mouth widened with shock as they pushed him up against the left hand wall and laid into him. I heard him gasp as punches knocked the air out of his lungs. Joshua was already doubled up as Nathan and Brandon rushed in too.

"Yes, get him!" Rebecca shouted.

"Teach him a lesson!" Sam yelled.

For a minute, I was like, totally stunned. Images of me surrounded by Emma and her thugs, my arms raised waiting for the attack flashed into my mind. This wasn't right, I couldn't do this.

"Stop!" I shouted, as Sapphire crept up beside me. She didn't speak, just nodded.

Trouble was, nobody heard me they were making so much noise with their grunting and shouting. Rebecca and the others had all edged forwards for a better view and stood cheering as Joshua groaned in pain.

My stomach tightened into a sick little ball. I'd caused this.

"Stop! I said stop!" I yelled as loud as I could, pushing my way through the girls then pulling the lads off, yelling in their ears. "Stop it! Leave him alone!"

At first they just shrugged me off, but that only made me more desperate.

"Stop it! Do you hear me? Stop it!"

I pulled and tugged, screaming at them until finally they listened and stood in stunned silence around me. I crouched down in front of Joshua, who'd sunk to the floor, his legs drawn up to his chest.

"Are you all right?" I asked then groaned inwardly. What a stupid, idiotic question. He'd just been battered by four lads, of course he wasn't all right. Duh! His nose was bleeding and his left eye was already swelling.

"Cow!" he hissed.

I winced.

"I'm sorry, Joshua, I didn't mean for this to happen."

"What're you apologising for, girl?" Sam's voice was filled with disgust. "He's the moron who mugged your gran. Don't you care anymore?"

I spun around, standing up as I did.

"Of course I care! Why do you think I organised all this? But I never actually wanted him beaten up. I just wanted to scare him."

"Nice time to tell us," said Jake, massaging the knuckles on this right hand. Even Sam was shaking her head.

"I'm sorry. It's my fault," I felt totally rotten. Like the smallest flea on the scruffiest dog in history. Luke was right. Things like this did get out of control. I should have listened to him.

I turned back to Joshua. "Look, Joshua. I hate what you did to Gran, but I shouldn't have organised this. It was wrong. Can I help you get home or something?"

I held out my hand but Joshua slapped it away.

"Just get out of my face!" he barked. He levered himself up against the wall, then pushed himself off. "You idiot! I never touched your stupid gran. Get it? Never!"

Then he barged past me and the others and walked away bent over slightly, his left hand holding his stomach.

My mind filled with doubts. What if he really hadn't done it and we'd just beaten up the wrong person? I felt so low, the worst person alive. After all I'd been through this year with Emma, I should've known better. And after what Luke told me about his trouble with bullies I'd got no right to do this. I wanted to take it all back, make it 'un-happen', but I couldn't. I couldn't do anything. I watched Joshua disappear up the alley and felt like I was drowning, huge waves crashing around me, carrying my gran away. I'd tried everything to rescue her, to get the fun loving mischievous Gran back, but I'd failed. She was being swept away to an old folk's home and she'd never be the same again.

Red hot anger burst up inside me and sprang out in scorching tears.

"My gran'll never be the same again because some LOSER decided it'd be a good idea to mug an old lady. But she's MY gran. MINE! I wish I'd got every one of them here. I could beat the truth out of them and find out who did it!"

I stomped around pulling at my hair in frustration. I felt so hopeless!

"But you just had one here and you let him go," Ruby said, her voice hard.

"I know!" I cried and flopped down on the hard, cold floor, suddenly empty of all energy. "Part of me wants to rage and hit and another part felt sick at the sight of you all hitting Joshua. I just don't know what to do!"

I buried my face in my hands. Everything was such a tangled mess, just like the fishing nets on the harbour. "I just want my gran to be okay and I don't know how to sort it. Why did somebody have to mug her? Why couldn't they just leave her alone?"

Nathan shook his head.

"Totally weird," he wrapped his arm around Ruby's shoulders. "Come on, babe, let's get out of here."

Ruby looked back over her shoulder as Nathan lead her away and called. "Ring you later." She smiled then turned away. Slowly the others with shuffling feet and not quite meeting my eyes, said 'see you' and walked away too until only Rebecca and Sam were left.

"I've been a complete idiot," I groaned. "After last time I should've known better. Violence doesn't solve anything. Luke was right. And now I've lost him as well."

"You might not have." Sam shrugged. "Ring him."

"Yeah, and like, say what?"

"What you've just said, that you're a complete idiot. That he was right and you don't deserve him..." Rebecca was ready to go on until I glared at her.

"All right, all right, no need to rub it in," I scowled, wiping my eyes with a tissue. "I know I've made a complete mess of everything. Anyway, I didn't hear either of you trying to stop me or coming up with any better ideas."

"Yeah, well, even perfect human beings have their limits." Sam flicked her plaits over her shoulders, her head high.

I groaned. Then fished out my mobile and speed dialed Luke. It rang then went to his voicemail.

"He's not answering."

I looked at my watch. It was only eleven, he should still be there. What if he'd gone early? I'd been so mean to him, I couldn't blame him. He'd probably never want to talk to me again.

174

"I've got to go see him," I said, scrambling up and heading down the alley, my footsteps echoing against the stark walls.

"Rach, it's too far, it'll take you too long. Get a taxi. We'll share." Rebecca suggested.

I knew she was right but I didn't want to wait. I paced up and down five metres of pavement, like I was trying to wear a groove in it. My head spun with all that'd happened and all I'd done. It was such a mess and I'd caused a lot of it.

When the black cab arrived, I was the first to open the door and climb inside.

"Queen's Parade," I said, while the others climbed in.

I watched the streets go by, my knees bouncing and my feet drumming a fast beat on the floor of the cab. I tried Luke's mobile every couple of minutes, but there was still no answer.

As soon as the cab pulled up, I flung the door wide and climbed out.

"Do you want me to come with...," Rebecca asked, leaning out of the taxi door.

I shook my head. There's no way I wanted a crowd watching me, this was gonna be hard enough as it was.

"Go for it, girl. Good luck," Sam said, leaning over Rebecca and looking up at me through the open door.

"Luck," said Rebecca. "Hope it goes okay."

"Me too," I said and shut the door. I handed the driver my part of the fare then turned to Luke's B & B. My stomach rolled as I looked up at the second story window belonging to Luke's room. Taking a deep breath, I crossed over the road and up the steps to the white door. I tried the handle but it was locked so I pressed the bell and waited. My hands tangled and untangled as I stared at the door, willing it to open. Finally a glazed figure appeared behind the frosted glass and it opened at last.

A slim woman of about fifty stood there, she wore a thin white cotton blouse and brown trousers with white smudges that looked like pastry.

"Can I help you?" she asked, her smile wide and welcoming.

"Could I see Luke Chambers, please?" I asked, my heart speeding up.

The smile vanished.

"Oh, I'm sorry, you're too late. Mr Chambers checked out."

"What?" My head spun. I felt like she'd hit me with a brick.

"He checked out," she glanced at her watch, "Oh, about half an hour ago."

"Where was he going?" My voice hardly came out my throat was so tight.

"Home, as far as I know. I think he said something about catching a train. Are you all right?" She looked down with a worried frown as I wobbled and held onto the wall.

"Erm, yeah, I'm okay. Erm, thanks."

My legs were suddenly so weak I had to go down the steps real slow. I could feel the landlady watching me so I walked up the road and onto the side street above before leaning back against the wall completely empty. Luke was gone, he hadn't waited.

I looked down at my watch, it was only 11.30. He'd gone an hour early! He must really hate me. He didn't even wait to see how it all went. But then he knew how it'd go, that's why he wouldn't join in. After

176

all I'd said and done I couldn't blame him for going. I deserved it. But it didn't stop me feeling sick.

Dragging my mobile out, I tried his number again, but slammed it back into my bag when the voice mail answered.

There was nothing I could do. Unless ... What if his train hadn't gone yet? I suddenly wished I hadn't let the cab go, there was no time to call another one.

I pushed off the wall and set off running, empowered by a glimmer of hope. Castle Road was pretty quiet but every so often I dodged an unsuspecting pedestrian.

My trainers pounded on the pavement and it wasn't long before my breath became deep and gasping. A woman pushed her buggy complete with toddler out of a shop, straight in front of me. With no time to dodge, I leapt into the air, landing with a thud on the other side. Cold tingles of shock prickled my body but I'd made it.

"Sorry!" I shouted back and kept right on running.

By the time I reached Northway my legs were screaming in pain, my chest hurt and it was real hard to breathe but I couldn't stop. I knew I'd see Luke when I got back to Rotherham but that was two weeks away. By then he'd have stewed on it more and he'd never forgive me, especially if he wouldn't accept my calls.

A pain shot through my right side just below my ribs. Stitch. Clamping my right hand onto it I kept running but it was getting harder and I knew I was slowing down. Finally I reached the junction and turned left, not far now. My lungs felt like balloons stretched so tight they were about to pop. I had to stop. I leaned against the wall and bent double, panting, my tongue hanging out like a dog. I knew people were staring at me as they walked past but I didn't care. I just had to get my breath back and set off again.

I didn't wait long. I was still panting when I started running again, but now my lungs didn't hurt quite as much. Shops disappeared fast as I ran past.

I finally reached the cross roads and joined a group of people waiting at the crossing.

"Come on," I urged, looking at the station on the opposite corner and chewing my lip, "Hurry up!"

It seemed an age before the lights changed and the cars stopped. As soon as they did I was the first across. Now only Westborough lay between me and the station. I wanted to scream at the cars to get out of my way. In my mind I could see Luke climbing onto the train and it setting off. He'd be gone, so angry and hurt and I'd never get chance to say sorry.

When the traffic finally stopped, I sprinted across, then over the zebra crossing on the station forecourt. I charged through the waiting area like a dog after a ball, dodging a couple of families with little kids and ran out onto the platform.

I'd never caught a train to Rotherham from Scarborough before, Dad drove us when we moved. So I'd no idea which platform I needed. I just stood there, frantically scanning left and right. There was no sign of Luke. A train was in. I swallowed. I looked back through the glass into the waiting area, in case I'd run past him, but there was no sign, so I jumped onto the train.

I pushed my way through carriage after carriage, squeezing around passengers and looking into every seat. I just hoped he wasn't in one of the toilets or I was well stuffed.

I went from one end of the train to the other but there was no sign of him.

'I'm too late. He's gone.' The thought drained every last gram of energy out of me. My body suddenly felt heavy all over like I'd put on loads of weight in a split second. Dragging myself off the train I headed for the nearest bench and flopped down onto it. I'd messed everything up. I'd failed Gran, she'd never be the same again. I'd got a boy beaten up, who'd probably want revenge now and I'd driven away the best boyfriend I was ever likely to have. I just wished I could go back to Rotherham and start the holidays all over again. This time I'd walk Gran home from the centre and none of this would happen. How could everything have gotten this bad?

"Rachel?"

I sucked in air and looked up.

Standing just to the right of me with his ruck sack slung over his broad shoulders was Luke.

"Luke?" I couldn't move, I just stared gormlessly up at him like he was a ghost or something.

We stayed like that just staring at each other not really knowing what to say until a family of five noisily rushed across the platform.

"Come on now!" the mother yelled. "Stop playing about or we'll miss the train!" She grabbed the arm of the youngest and yanked him towards the waiting train.

Luke looked at his watch.

"I've got to go." He turned away.

"Luke. Wait." I jumped up and caught his arm. "Please don't go."

"I thought you wanted me to." Luke's voice was flat, his eyes accusing.

"No, I don't. I'm sorry, I was stupid. You were right. It got out of hand and Joshua got hurt. But I stopped them and told them to leave him alone. I don't

179

want to get like him. I know I was wrong and I won't be going after Joshua any more. I'm not even sure he did it." I shook my head. "I don't know how to help Gran now. Maybe I can't."

Luke met my gaze and my heart ripped in half at the sadness there.

"It isn't just about Joshua and your gran," he said.

My head dropped. I sucked in my lips and wondered how to start.

"I'm sorry I never listen to you. I said such mean things, when you were only trying to help." I looked up at him, my eyes pleading. "I'm really am sorry. I should have trusted you."

"This isn't the first time," Luke said, quietly. "It's like you only want me if I'm going to agree with you all the time. Well, I'm not. I've got my own opinions and if you can't handle that then there's no point us being together."

My cheeks burned.

"I don't know what to say, except that I'm an idiot and I know it now. I promise I'll listen to everything you say from now on."

"No, you won't." Luke's voice was still flat, but a little smile played around his lips.

"Maybe I will." I tried what I hoped was a cheeky smile. "I'll try."

"Yeah, sure," Luke grimaced, "Like Brittany tries to sing."

"She can sing!" I protested.

"Yeah, right," Luke said, as the train doors closed. Luke watched them. "Looks like I missed my train."

I nodded.

"Do you, erm, want to come back to Gran's?"

"I might as well. I've got no B & B to go to and I'm starving. Any chance of a fry up or summat?" Luke hitched his ruck sack higher onto his shoulders.

I grinned. "Yeah, if you want to risk my cooking."

"We've all got to die of summat." Luke shrugged.

I thumped him on the arm, a warm feeling spreading from my heart right through my body. We were back and from now on I was gonna think twice before I opened my mouth.

Luke slipped his arm around my shoulders and we walked over to Gran's talking about us and about Joshua. By the time we got there, neither of us had come up with anything that would help Gran. I felt good being with Luke again but there was a heaviness in my heart that just wouldn't go away.

I walked down the short path to the front door and turned the handle. It was locked. I pulled the key from my bag but before I could slip it into the lock, I heard a shout from inside.

"Shut up!" A male voice boomed from the sitting room.

I froze, a cold knife piercing my heart.

Luke saw me hesitate. "What's up?"

"Joshua's here," I whispered. I looked at Luke, fear trickling down my spine like rain water. "It's my fault. He's come for revenge because of me."

Luke swallowed. "What shall we do?"

"I don't know."

I crept up to the sitting room window, cursing when my jacket snagged on the rose bush growing along the wall. I quietly pried it loose then sidled up to the window my heart beating so loud I was sure they'd hear it through the glass.

181

I stood facing the wall just to the left of the window then slowly leaned to my right so that just one eye peeped out beyond the wall. The net curtain hung like a white cloud blocking my vision. Scanning it, I found a small gap in the pattern and peered through. It was like trying to see through a sweet wrapper.

I could only make out vague shapes. One was small, sitting huddled in the rocking chair, I could only see her profile but knew it was Gran. Another was taller but slim, dressed all in blue and standing beside Gran, one arm protectively on the chair back. She was facing away from me, but I knew it was Rebecca.

I squinted trying to see further into the room in the direction Gran and Rebecca were staring. The figure was large, waving something shiny in his hand.

It wasn't Joshua, it was too big.

The figure stepped closer. My throat closed up. I knew who it was, I'd seen that person before.

This was bad. Very bad.

CHAPTER SEVENTEEN

I rolled away from the window so that my back leaned against the wall.

"What is it? What did you see?" Luke edged closer.

I just stood there shaking my head, my eyes closed.

"It can't be, I don't believe it," I muttered.

"Rachel, what is it?" Luke demanded. "You're seriously worrying me now."

Trying to ignore the desperate heaviness inside my chest, I pulled myself away from the prickly rose thorns and led Luke away from the window.

"It isn't Joshua," I whispered.

"Not Joshua? Then who?" The wind whipped Luke's hair as he waited for me to answer. He ran his hand through it, a frown on his face.

Shaking my head again, I said, "It's Mark."

"Who?"

"The bull. My brother, Mark."

Luke's eyes widened. "The Neanderthal?"

"Yeah and it looks like he's got a knife." My voice was level, almost dead. I felt like we'd already lost.

"We've got to call the police then." Luke's voice was firm, decisive.

I nodded and followed him out onto the pavement, so we wouldn't be heard. Luke made the call. My throat was too tight for me to speak. I just stood there staring at the bungalow his words washing over me like waves. My gran and twin sister were in there being threatened with a knife. I had to help them somehow. My eyes fixed on Gran's open bedroom window and an idea formed.

"I've got to get in there," I said when Luke's call ended.

"No way! You're not going in there. You'll be killed. I mean, do you need your head reading or summat?"

I caught Luke's arm, my grip and voice firm.

"It's my fault he's here. I went to his house. I've got to go in. If the police go knocking on the door or storming in there, he could do something stupid. Look, I don't know him or what he's capable of, but I do know he's big and strong and cocky. Marcy was virtually cowering away from him at the house."

"That's another reason for you not to go in." Luke took my hand off his arm and held it.

"I know, Luke, but I've got to do something. Look, Gran's bedroom window is open, I reckon I can open it a bit wider and get in. I'll keep quiet and out of the way unless they're in immediate danger."

"And if they are in danger, you're going to do what exactly?"

I shrugged.

"I don't know. I just know I've got to be in there just in case. I'm not leaving them alone, Luke."

Luke's shoulders sagged. "Okay. But I still think you're crazy."

I nodded. Neither of us had mentioned Luke coming in with me because one look at the window showed there was no way Luke'd squeeze through it. Even I was gonna have to really hold my breath to have any chance of fitting through.

We crept over to the window. Luke took my face in both hands and kissed me, hard.

"You be careful in there," he said, his voice thick with emotion.

I nodded. My throat was squeezed so tight no words would come out.

Luke gave me a tight smile then knelt down and I stepped up onto his back. He groaned quietly when I brought my second foot up and right then I decided I needed to go on a diet. Not a major one, just enough to lose a couple of kilograms. I shook my head, this was not the time to think about diets!

Reaching my hand under the glass, I unhooked the latch and pulled the window further towards me, as far as it would go. Standing on tiptoe, I squeezed my head and shoulders inside then wriggled in up to my waist, pulling myself up as I went. My feet left Luke's back and he stood up with a soft groan as the window frame bit into my stomach. Right in the middle there was a metal bit that the latch was supposed to fasten on to. It'd stuck right into my belly button and was killing me. I was having a really hard time not groaning out loud.

"Help me, Luke," I hissed. Then felt a bit easier when Luke's hands grabbed my feet and pushed gently upwards. I slithered further in, trying to push myself up with my hands so that the metal bit didn't scratch all the way down my front. Finally there were only my legs dangling outside. I hung upside down trying to reach far enough to rest my hands on the chest of drawers. I could see Luke outside, holding onto my ankles to stop me sliding all the way in too soon. Mark's angry voice boomed from the sitting room. He was shouting something, but with the door to the bedroom closed it was too muffled and I couldn't make out the words.

My hands finally reached the chest of drawers but as I put my weight down my wrist caught a little girl ornament. It wobbled and my heart almost stopped as I tried to grab it before it fell to the floor. I caught it in my right hand and held tight. I breathed again, but not easily, my chest and stomach felt stretched beyond their limits, like I was trying to squeeze into jeans that were way too small. Now that I was upside down, hands on the drawers I didn't know what to do next. The ornaments were in the way and there was no where nearby to put them. If I brought my feet down now, I was gonna end up falling head first onto the floor.

I felt like such an idiot. What had I thought I was doing? Trouble was I couldn't go back. I mean, even if Luke could pull me back up, my stomach would scrape over that metal sticky up thing and I didn't want that pain again. There was no option I'd got to keep going. Very carefully I moved each ornament, two girls in frilly pink dresses, a boy with a horse and an old lady in a rocking chair, over to the right of the cabinet. Then I wriggled further in. My arms took all my weight and shook with the strain. Why didn't I work out? A bit of muscle would really come in handy right now.

'Hold on Rachel, hold on.' I told myself, feeling pressure building up in my face from the blood rushing to my head. My elbows were ready to give way as I managed to get my left leg inside. I brought it down as quickly as I could and sighed with relief when my trainer touched the top of the drawers. Steadying myself I brought my right leg down so I was standing on all fours on the cupboard.

Taking a deep breath, I slowly lowered myself to my knees then climbed down, one leg at a time. When I finally stood inside looking out at Luke my limbs felt like jelly.

"Are you okay?" he mouthed.

I nodded.

"I'll go watch for the police," he mouthed. Then blew a kiss and winked before turning away.

I watched him walk away suddenly feeling very alone. I knew the others were in the sitting room, but here in the bedroom I was on my own and I hadn't a clue what to do next. I sighed. I had to do something. My palms were really sweaty as I crept over to the door and leaned my ear against it. The brother was still spouting off. I closed my eyes, picturing Gran's hall. If I opened this door, Gran and Rebecca would probably see me, but Mark shouldn't, unless he'd moved.

A scraping noise filled my ears as I ground my teeth trying to work out what to do. If I opened the door and he saw me, I'd be captured just like them. If he didn't see me, I might be able to do something, though I'd no idea what. At least I'd be able to hear what was going on. If I just stayed in the bedroom I was no use to anybody. So, there was no choice.

Putting my hand on the door knob, I turned it real slow, holding my breath, hoping it wouldn't squeak. Then I eased it open just enough for one eye to peep out.

Mark was standing just inside the sitting room. He was so broad he just about filled the opening. I couldn't see Rebecca or Gran, but now I could hear what was going on.

"Now stay there!" He pointed the knife in Rebecca's direction.

"Who are you?" Rebecca's shaky voice asked. "What do you want?"

"You know who I am and look at her face, she knows as well." Mark laughed into the silence, "Come on, put it together!"

I frowned, Mark thought Rebecca was me and should know him but why would Gran know who he was?

Suddenly a light flicked on in my brain and I gasped aloud then clamped my hand over my mouth in fear. I dodged back behind the door holding my breath and hoping I hadn't given myself away. I listened for movement but when nothing happened I peeped back around the door as Rebecca's voice, filled with loathing seeped out into the hall.

"You're the brother and you're the one who hurt Gran."

Mark clapped. "Give the girl a prize."

"But why did you hurt her? What's she ever done to you?"

"She didn't do anything. You and that twin of yours did it all. I hate you!" He spat out the words and my stomach clenched.

"But what did we do? We were just babies when she got rid of us."

"You ruined my life!" Mark snarled, "And you're still ruining it!"

"But how? We haven't seen you for years."

Rebecca was asking the same questions that swam in my mind. What damage could two babies have done? And how did Gran fit into all this?

"You got born, that's how."

"That's just stupid." Rebecca's voice oosed scorn.

"Don't call me stupid!" Mark strode further into the room his right arm extended, brandishing the knife. "You want to know what you did? I'll tell you. Then you'll know why I've got to do what I'm gonna do. Before you were born everything was good."

"Your dad used to beat your mum." Rebecca's voice shot out.

'*Quiet, Rebecca,*' I silently urged. She'd obviously regained her confidence.

"Dad said they'd got an understanding. They were okay. If he hit her, she made him do it."

"She *made* him hit her?" Rebecca snorted. "What planet are you from? Nobody *makes* somebody hurt them. Your dad hurt her because he's an alcho' and a bully and you're just like him!"

I closed my eyes. Why couldn't Rebecca just keep her mouth shut for once?

"You shut up about my dad!" Mark shouted, lurching forwards. He stood only a metre away from them now. "You know nothing about him. You and that sister of yours are just trouble."

I could hear the hate in Mark's voice as he spoke. "Mother always had time for me before you two came along. We did all sorts together. After you came she was always too busy and Dad shouted loads more, he hated you and so did I. But I got rid of you!"

I frowned. What did he mean? Marcy said she got rid of us to keep us safe from the dad.

"I'd go into your room and nip your ugly pink bodies. You'd scream and Dad'd get mad. Mother'd come running in, panicking like crazy. I used to hide in the room and watch her rock you and sing songs to shut you up. Finally she got rid of you both and had more time for me again. It should've been fantastic, but she kept upsetting Dad and made him hurt her again."

I heard Rebecca grunt in disgust but thankfully Mark didn't seem to notice he just ranted on. It was like he'd finally got the chance to let out his rage and it was all gushing out like blood from a ruptured artery.

"When I was ten she got Dad put in prison and I ended up in foster care. Their son was older than me and a bully, he used to cause trouble and blame me. His parents always believed him, they thought he was a frickin' angel! When Mother came for me she took me to a tiny flat in Sheffield, said she couldn't pay the mortgage on the house. While she worked and went to nursing college I was forever with one stupid sitter or another. After that she dragged me all over the country. We never stayed anywhere long enough to make friends. *'I've got to find my girls,'* she kept saying," his voice was mocking. "She was obsessed. She nearly exploded with joy when she got a job at Doncaster hospital and spotted that ugly twin of yours."

I heard Rebecca gasp.

"She even took a picture, carries it everywhere in her purse, like it's made of gold or summat. Took her a couple of weeks to check and be sure it was one of 'her girls' but by then the twin'd emigrated." He laughed. "Serves her right."

So Marcy had been fooled by the emigration thing just like me when I looked for Rebecca. The new house owner said they'd emigrated with no forwarding address but they didn't. When I checked further I found out that Rebecca's parents separated and never went abroad. All they did was move house. Rebecca ended up in Swinton, near Rotherham where I found her.

"Then she moved us to Scarborough to find you. But she was too late again. Instead she found the old bag. Told me where she lives and everything. I came to look but she was just this boring old woman. Then a couple of weeks ago I saw you both going to that old crock's place. I knew straight away who you were, the old bag and the identical twin. Mother's shown me that

190

stupid photo so often you couldn't be anybody else. This was my chance, I was gonna frighten you so bad you'd never come back to Scarborough again. But no, you had to get straight into that taxi, didn't you?"

My fists tightened. I knew what was coming and my insides were squeezing up like they were in a vice. Every time he called Gran an 'old bag' they squeezed up even more. I wanted to jump out and hit him until all the anger and frustration I'd felt this last few weeks had all poured out.

I couldn't see Gran from where I stood but I was really hoping something was stirring in her. The Gran she used to be would've been giving him 'what for' as she used to say, but right now, she was silent. My stomach twisted, hoping this wasn't making her worse. I pictured her cowering in the rocking chair, fear etched on her precious face.

"I waited for you to come back for the old bag," he went on, "But you had to spoil that as well, didn't you? So, when you never came, I decided to put *her* out of action instead."

"Why? She's never done anything to you!" Rebecca spat out the question that'd tormented my brain for weeks.

Mark laughed. "So? What difference does that make? With her in hospital you'd have no where to stay. You'd have to go home. Then knowing Mother she'd move us away before you had chance to come and visit again. It would've worked as well but you had to go and bump into Mother at the hospital. Of all the frickin' nurses there you had to bump into her! Then you turn up at our house like you own it! You've left me with no choice. Dad'll be out of prison soon and I'm not gonna let you get in the way of him getting back with Mother. She's got her own house now so we can stay here and be a family again."

"Get real. There's no way that's gonna happen!" Rebecca declared, her voice laced with scorn. "If she's any sense she won't even look at a bully like him. The best thing she did was have him locked up!"

I shook my head, *'Way to go, Rebecca. Wind him up some more, why don't you?'*

"Yeah, well you'll never know, will you?" he snarled, his voice rising. "With one twin in another country, there's only you and the old bag to spoil it and I'm gonna make sure you never spoil anything ever again!"

He lurched forwards, the knife raised. Gran screamed.

Helplessness flooded my body. I'd got to do something and now, but what?

CHAPTER EIGHTEEN

I scanned the room for inspiration, something, anything that would help. My eyes rested on the ornaments on the set of drawers. Running across the room I grabbed one of the little girls, muttering, "Sorry, Gran," and ran back to the door. I was just in time to see Rebecca dodge Mark's attack, his knife missing her by a tiny fraction.

"Okay, come and get me if you can!" Rebecca yelled, taunting him as she ran across the room behind the settee, drawing him away from Gran.

Gran sat huddled in the rocking chair her arms wrapped tightly around her. Her face was as white as a full moon with wide frightened eyes. Mark growled in frustration then spun around and charged after Rebecca. With only a second to think, I ran out into the hall, hid behind the wall to the left of the sitting room door then threw the ornament as hard as I could against the opposite wall. With a loud CRASH, it splintered into like, a million tiny fragments and scattered all over the floor.

I couldn't see what'd happened in the room, I just hoped Mark'd turned away from Rebecca.

Then I heard his lumbering steps heading for the door. My heart slammed into my rib cage harder than the ornament had just hit the wall. What was I doing? He was coming after me now. Like, great plan Rachel!

It must've only been seconds but it seemed like forever. I heard every step pounding my way, like it was in slow motion or something. I could feel the vibrations in the wall and when they finally reached the doorway I did the only thing my panicked brain could think of ... I stuck out my leg.

Mark crashed into it and pain seered through my ankle like a red hot poker. I cried out in pain as Mark fell forwards.

Rebecca appeared in the doorway beside me as Mark's hands hit the opposite wall and he steadied himself.

When he turned his face was bright red like he'd spent too long in the sun. He'd got a crazed look in his eyes and was growling like a mad dog. The stench of booze as he spun around was so strong it was like being hit by a solid wall of alcohol.

"Both of you!" he snarled. "Now you're both gonna die!"

He lunged forwards. Rebecca jumped to the left and I jumped to the right. Mark stumbled through the doorway into the sitting room. I wasn't gonna let him get anywhere near Gran though so I spun around and jumped on his back. It was like riding a wild horse. He heaved up then ducked low trying to shake me off. His gigantic hands swung around trying to grab me, the knife dangerously close to my arm. Rebecca followed me in and dived for his legs. She grabbed them and held on. Mark struggled and wobbled but he didn't go down. He was as strong as a bull, there was no stopping him.

Suddenly Mark caught hold of my right arm. He pulled hard and I lost my grip. I slid off his back and landed on the floor by his feet. I watched his face break into a grin as he raised his arm, the knife glinting in the light from Gran's reading lamp. From the corner of my eye I could see Rebecca's face frozen in horror. She still clung to his legs but was helpless to stop him.

Right then I knew I would die. There was nothing anybody could do.

I watched the blade streak down towards me, it filled my vision. There was only me and that knife, nothing else. I didn't even hear the crash. Splinters of china showered down on me like rain. The knife momentarily froze then dropped harmlessly beside me as Mark collapsed like a felled tree.

Rebecca scrambled to her knees looking above my head. I followed her gaze and there was Gran, standing on her tip toes with the remains of her best china vase in her hands.

"Nobody hurts my grandchildren!" She said, her eyes glinting and her lips pursed.

I stared at her for a minute, stunned then pushed myself up into a sitting position.

"Way to go, Gran!" I said, like, totally amazed. The scared, nervous old woman'd gone and my gran stood there the old determination back in her face.

Finally she dropped her arms and the bottom of the vase landed on the carpet with a gentle thud, just as the sound of sirens seeped into the room.

"Is he dead?" Gran stared down at him.

I didn't really want to touch him, but for Gran's sake I put two fingers on his neck beside his wind pipe.

"Nah, his heart's still pumping," I said, "Funny that, I didn't think he'd got one."

Rebecca sniggered.

"Gran, I can't believe you saved me," I said, my hands still shaking as I moved away from Mark.

"It was a team effort," Gran said, smiling. "My two girls and me."

At that both me and Rebecca scrambled up and flung our arms around her neck.

"Thanks, Gran!" We both echoed, hugging her tight

"You're one tough cookie," I said, grinning, tears of relief running down my cheeks.

"Hey, I think we'd better let the police in." Rebecca pulled away and that's when I noticed the sirens had stopped and the room was filled with flashing blue light.

"Yeah, we'd better, before they bash the door down," I answered.

"Oh, yes," Gran said, quickly. "Let them in, Love. I don't want a broken door!"

Rebecca stepped over Mark, still laying out cold on the floor and jogged into the hall. I heard the front door being unlocked then two big figures in blue appeared framed in the sitting room doorway. The young one was a real hotty! They both stood there staring down at Mark's fat body laying like a beached whale on Gran's flowered carpet.

"So, who's responsible for this then?" The older copper said, as Luke's head appeared over his shoulder.

"I thought we asked you to wait outside," the younger one said to Luke.

"I couldn't wait out there, Rachel could've been hurt," Luke said, a small frown creasing his perfect forehead. He was definitely hotter than the copper.

A tidal wave of love shot up from my toes and exploded out through my arms as I jumped over Mark and launched myself at Luke, knocking the two policemen out of the way.

"All right, you two," the older policeman said, with a slight smile as mine and Luke's lips got friendly, our arms locked around each other. "Now, like I said, who's responsible for this?" He nodded down at Mark again, like we'd forgotten he was there or something.

196

Reluctantly unhooking my lips, I looked over my shoulder.

"Gran did it," I said.

Gran blushed and hung her head.

"Only cos he was gonna kill us," said Rebecca.

"Yeah, he had a knife," I added.

"He was gonna stab her," Rebecca, jumped in.

"I couldn't let him hurt my girls," Gran said, defensively.

"He was gonna stab Rebecca as well," I said

"Yeah, he chased me across the room."

"So I chucked an ornament against the wall."

"And she tripped him up when he ran out," Rebecca added.

"He was going to stab Rachel, you see," Gran said. "I had no choice."

"Rachel?" Luke's eyes widened, his arm tightening around me.

"Well, he pulled me off his back and ..."

"Whoa!" The older policeman held up his hands. "One at a time, please. Let's allow the ambulance crew to attend to this young man, Pc Corbett, call it in, we'll need someone to accompany this young gent to the hospital. Then the rest of us can sit down and one at a time you can tell me what happened here. From the beginning."

So that's how we spent the next two hours. First the ambulance crew came in, declared Mark curable and carted him off to the hospital. Then we took it in turns to tell the policemen what had happened.

"We will, of course, need to speak to your parents."

My breath caught and I looked across at Rebecca and Luke whose eyes were as wide as mine.

"Do you have to?" I almost whispered.

"I'm afraid so," he said, "Why? Is there any reason you would prefer I didn't?"

"Er, well." I shot a look at Rebecca. I mean, of course there was no reason, except that Mum had no idea that Gran had even been mugged, never mind about me meeting my birth mother and psychotic older brother. She was only gonna go, like, totally mental. Then there was Rebecca's mother, she'd only just found out that Rebecca and me were in touch. She'd probably think I'm a bad influence or something and tell Rebecca to go straight home and never see me again. And Luke's mum ... well, she totally freaked last time, she'd go into a proper melt down now. So, yeah, totally great idea to ring them, no problem at all. "I suppose not," I said.

"Right then. I presume Rachel's parents are still away?"

He raised his eyebrows at Gran. I willed her to say yes, but she shook her head.

"No, they are back now, you can ring them."

I frowned. Why the change?

"Very well, we'll need you to come down to the station and make formal statements."

"Now?" I asked, looking at Gran.

"No, tomorrow will be fine," the officer answered.

Gran stood. "That will not be a problem officer," she said and shook his hand.

I stared, my mouth gaping. Had I heard right? I glanced at Luke and Rebecca who were both grinning and gradually I smiled too. Gran was back to her old self. Whacking Mark on the head defending her granddaughters had totally cured her. I know Rebecca wasn't technically her granddaughter but it felt good to think of her that way, it sort of made our being sisters official. Everything was good again.

Instantly, an image exploded into my head and the smile dropped off my face. Joshua Green. A lump the size of a football lodged in my throat. I'd hounded him and had him beaten up and he hadn't done anything, apart from being a total perv on that first day.

It was Mark who'd hurt Gran, not Joshua, so all this time he'd been telling the truth. He was innocent. Well, maybe that's not quite the right word for Joshua. But anyway, he didn't do this.

My head was like, spinning. I was like, *'hey, stop the world a minute I want to get off and get my head straight'*. But, of course, that didn't happen. Instead the policemen left and the four of us just sat there staring at each other in total silence. Then suddenly we all started talking and couldn't stop. We went over it all again and again. We congratulated Gran. Rebecca and Gran thanked me. I blushed and said it was nothing. Luke asked all sorts of questions, he wanted to know every detail.

Gran said she'd never known her attacker's name. She presumed this Joshua Green we were pursuing was the right person and she was terrified for my safety. After Mark had knocked her down he grabbed her arm and broken it saying he'd do the same to my neck if she said anything. Then he snatched her bag and ran. It was never meant to be a mugging it was actually an outpouring of Mark's rage against the twins he thought ruined his life. If I'd only collected Gran it would've been me he attacked instead of her.

My head was seriously hurting when an hour later the shrill ringing of the telephone interrupted us. Me, Rebecca and Luke all locked eyes. Which parent was it?

Even Gran didn't move. She just sat there gently rocking, looking anywhere in the room except at us. I sighed and went to answer it, dragging my feet like a condemned criminal.

"Hello?"

"Rachel, is that you?" It was Mum's voice. I closed my eyes. "I've just had the police on the phone. What's all this about your gran being mugged and you all being attacked by this Mark person? And why am I hearing about it now for the first time? Just how long has all this been going on? Why didn't you tell me? Are you all okay? What happened?"

I groaned on the inside. I'd got no idea which question to answer first.

After spending nearly an hour on the phone, Mum announced she was coming straight through.

Rebecca and Luke both got calls on their mobiles while I was on the phone and from the looks on their faces it wasn't going well.

"We've got to go home tomorrow after we've given our statements," they both announced once I was free.

My shoulders sagged, I'd really wanted them around a bit longer, especially Luke. He'd only been here four days and if he left tomorrow I'd have to wait nearly a week before seeing him again. We'd only just made up, it was way too soon to be apart.

***

Just over an hour and a half later, Dad's car screeched to a stop outside Gran's. He must have broken just about every speed limit to get here that quick. Mum was straight out of the car and into Gran's like a greyhound out of the traps.

200

"Rachel? Mother?" She marched in, her eyes flicking left and right. She spotted me first, just coming out of the sitting room to meet her. She launched herself at me and suddenly my face was pressed against her chest so hard I couldn't breathe. "Rachel, are you all right?"

"I'mph fine," I muttered from inside the white cotton of her blouse.

Thankfully at that minute Mum spotted Gran. She released me and treated Gran to the same hug she'd just given me.

"I reckon she's relieved you're all right," Rebecca's voice whispered in my ear.

"Just a bit," I whispered back. I've got to admit though, Mum was as white as her blouse. I did feel, sort of, sorry for her. I mean, I know what's it's like being kept in the dark, not knowing what's really going on and it's not good.

Dad walked in and looked down at me, his brown eyes leaking concern.

"We're all right, Dad," I said without him asking.

He nodded, put his arm around my shoulders and squeezed then led me back into the sitting room. We all found seats, Luke, me and Rebecca on the settee, Gran in her rocker and Mum and Dad in the two arm chairs.

Then we had to go through everything again with Mum and Dad stopping us every now and again to ask questions.

Dad was pretty laid back about everything, like he said, "It's all over now so there's no point getting worked up about it."

Mum didn't agree and decided she was gonna stay for the rest of my visit and keep an eye on us.

The next day, I stood beside Luke and Rebecca on the train station platform.

"It's not gonna be the same around here without you two," I said.

"Oh, thanks a bunch!" Sam frowned beside me. She'd spent just about every minute with us once I'd texted what happened. She'd only gone home the night before to sleep then came straight back.

"It's only for a week. You're coming back on Monday, aren't you?" Luke asked, ignoring Sam.

I nodded.

"I'm glad your Gran's gonna be okay," Rebecca said.

"Yeah. Mum's gonna stay with her for a few weeks and get her out a bit more everyday until she can go out on her own again." I paused. "I'm glad Mum's here, it's like, I can relax a bit now because she's taking care of things. She'll make sure Gran's okay."

"She'll be all right," Sam said, one hand on her hip. "Your Gran's a tough old bird. Anyway, I'm not going anywhere, unlike you lot. I'll be here and I'll keep an eye on her, even after your mum's gone home."

Warm gratitude flooded me.

"Thanks, Sam that makes me feel loads better."

"All part of the service." She bowed and waggled her hand in a royal wave.

"Are you sure you won't meet Marcy?" I turned to Rebecca, trying one last time.

"I've already told you. No." Rebecca's jaw set, "I know all you've said about it not being her fault and all that. But she had her choices. She could've done it different. I just don't want anything to do with her."

Something ached inside me, I just wanted them to meet, to give each other a chance, for both their sakes. Meeting Marcy didn't make my world perfect or anything, but it had filled in a few gaps.

"Well, we'd better go," Luke glanced at the train whose engines had just fired up.

I nodded, feeling like my heart was blocking my throat. I stood on tiptoe and kissed him. He kissed back sending chills down my spine. His arms slipped around my back and pulled me against the warmth of his body. No matter what'd happened earlier, in his arms I felt safe as though the world couldn't touch me.

"Ugh, get a room you two." Rebecca made a gagging noise. "I'm gonna puke."

Luke's grip loosened and I frowned at Rebecca.

"What did I do?" she asked, looking all innocent.

"See you soon," Luke almost whispered.

"Count on it," I said, giving him a last grin before they headed for the train.

"Have a good last week!" Luke called.

"An uneventful one!" added Rebecca, wagging her finger at me.

"Well, it won't be entirely uneventful." I grimaced. "There's two people I've got to see before I go and I'm not looking forward to seeing either of them."

CHAPTER NINETEEN

It was the next morning before I plucked up enough courage to see the first one.

"You sure you want to go through with this?" The look on Sam's face told me she thought I was being a complete idiot.

I sighed. "I don't *want* to do it, but I've got to."

Sam shrugged. "I don't see why, but whatever. Do you want me to come?"

"No, just hang about here in case I need you."

"Well, if he tries anything shout, okay?"

I nodded. "Yeah, okay."

I drew in a massive breath, then turned and walked down the road towards Joshua's house. It was cold but sweat clung to my forehead. My stomach was swimming and I wished I hadn't eaten cereal for breakfast. In fact, I wished I hadn't eaten breakfast at all.

By the time I reached Joshua's door I felt real sick. Swallowing hard, I knocked.

"Who is it?" A muffled female voice called out.

"Is Joshua there, please?" I said, avoiding the question. I didn't want Joshua refusing to come to the door.

I shuffled my feet on their soggy welcome mat wishing I could be anywhere but here. When the door opened to say Joshua looked shocked would be like saying super models look a bit thin. His mouth dropped and his one good eye opened so wide it looked like his eyeball might drop out. The other was swollen tight

shut making my stomach flip over with guilt. Finally
he clamped his lips together real tight so they turned
white and his fists clenched.

"What're *you* doing here?"

"I came to apologise." I couldn't look at him, his
closed eye and bruised face just made me feel worse.
Instead I stared at his bare feet planted squarely on the
brown lino.

"You did that already. So get lost. If you're
looking for forgiveness go to a priest or somethin',
you're not getting it here." His feet turned. I looked
up, speaking quickly before the door closed in my face.

"But I know you were telling the truth!"

Joshua hesitated then turned back to me.

"Oh, yeah?"

I nodded. "Look, I really am sorry. I know who
did it now. I know it wasn't you. What we did to you,
it was wrong. I don't know what to say except, I'm
sorry."

"Yeah? Well sorry won't get rid of this black
eye will it? So, like I said, just get lost. Go back to
Rotherham or whatever rock you've gone to live under
and don't bother coming back."

He spun around and the door slammed shut.

My heart pounded. I'd known he wouldn't be
glad to see me but I'd hoped it'd go better than that. I
raised my arm, tempted to knock again, but changed my
mind. I mean, what did I want from him anyway,
absolution or something? Was I doing this for him or
me? I'd said sorry and that'd have to be it, there was
nothing else I could do, like he said, I couldn't take
back the bruises, could I? What I'd done was so wrong
and against my real nature, I guess I just wanted to feel
better about myself. I'd just have to make sure that

from now on I listen to people and not judge them without any facts. And definitely no more violence!

Turning away, I headed back to the street and across to Sam.

"How'd it go?" she asked.

I shrugged. "Rubbish, I guess, but I've done it. I've said sorry, so that'll have to be it."

We walked down the road side by side.

"So, do you fancy a day on the beach?" I looked at Sam hopefully.

She grimaced. "But it's cold and wet. What do you want, pneumonia or summat?"

"No, just a few laughs with my friends before I've got to go again."

Sam, grinned. "Okay, you've got it. I'll text the others."

Within an hour Sam, Summer, Ruby, Sapphire and me were on the beach. It was too cold for sun bathing, but the sand had already dried out after a night of rain, so we spent the day burying each other fully dressed in the sand, paddling in the sea and pigging out on hot dogs, fish and chips and prawns. It was a fantastic day and I arranged to meet up with them again the next afternoon. I already had plans for the morning.

I spent the evening in with Gran, Sam and my mum. We played Scrabble and Gran was up to her old tricks, making up weird words and pretending to be surprised that we didn't know them. Her best was Zebroo on a triple word score. She tried to convince us it was a cross between a zebra and a kangaroo made in an experiment in Australia. We were having none of it! But it was great to see the mischief back in her eyes. I think standing up to Mark and knowing he was locked up had given her back all her confidence. I watched her with tongue in cheek studying her letter tray, probably trying to figure out another cheat.

"Rachel, it's your move. Rachel?" Mum's voice broke through.

"Ugh?" I said, intelligently, trying to drag my mind back to the game.

"It's your move."

"Oh." I looked down at my letters as Sam rolled her eyes, shaking her head.

I just gave her a 'don't start' look and went back to figuring out my next word.

I was totally shattered when I went to bed that night, especially when I thought about what I'd got to do the next day. I just hoped that it'd go better than the visit with Joshua.

***

I didn't sleep much. Mum had my bed so I got Rebecca's camp bed. It wasn't comfy! How on earth she'd slept on it for four nights I don't know. Great black shadows hung under my eyes like hammocks the next morning. Wrinkling my nose I reached for my makeup bag and ten minutes later looked almost human.

I could smell bacon and eggs and followed my nose into the kitchen. Mum stood over the frying pan prodding the bacon with a spatula and Gran was setting the table.

"Looks like you two have been busy. Is there anything I can do?" I felt really guilty sleeping in while they were up and working.

"No, you just sit yourself down there, it's all ready." Gran pointed with a flowered mug and I obediently sat down. It was so good having Gran all confident again, there was no way I was gonna disagree with her about anything.

Soon Mum and Gran joined me and we had this like, family breakfast, all happy and chatty. They even managed to wake me up a bit and temporarily forget what I had to do. Unfortunately breakfast didn't last forever and sighing, I stood and put my pots in the sink.

"I've got to go out for a bit. Do you want me to wash these first seeing as you two did the cooking?" I asked.

"Why not," Mum said before Gran had chance.

About half hour later I climbed onto a brown and cream single decker bus. Sitting near the front I stared out the window watching the houses go by.

My fingers were locked together and pressed against my stomach, trying to calm it down. This was something I had to do before going home but I'd got no idea how I'd be received, I mean, I'd just sent her son to prison.

I stepped down off the bus outside the hospital and tried to remember the way to Marcy's house. For the first time I was nervous about whether I'd even find it again! When I reached a street of semi-detached houses and spotted one, about half way down, with blue curtains, I knew I was in the right place. Walking over, I gulped as I knocked on the door.

The door opened within a minute and Marcy's face appeared, grey and frowning.

"Rachel!"

"Hello?" I said, hardly daring to look at her.

"I'm sorry ..." We both began then looked at each other in surprise.

"I'm sorry your son's in prison because of me," I continued.

"No." Marcy's eyes were wide. "I'm the one who's sorry. Sorry that I couldn't control Mark and for all he went through as a child that turned him into ... well ... a duplicate of his father. And I'm so sorry for what he did to your gran." She sobbed and bit her lip. "I can't believe he tried to kill you. How can you ever forgive me?"

Marcy's eyes were fixed on mine, like deep pools pleading for mercy.

"It wasn't your fault," I said, quickly. "I mean, if I hadn't shown up again none of this would've happened."

"Rachel, all you did was visit your gran. I'm the one who moved here to find you and told Mark where your gran lives. I thought he was upset because the family was separated. I actually thought he'd be pleased to be a step closer to finding you." She shook her head. "I never imagined he'd do anything like that. How can a mother be so wrong?"

I didn't really know what to say, I mean, she wasn't exactly in line for any 'Mother of the Year' awards, but she looked so miserable. I had to say something.

"It was nice of you to try and find me."

Marcy's face relaxed a bit and she smiled. "It's kind of you to say that. Do want to come in?"

I nodded.

Marcy led the way inside and through to the kitchen. She instinctively filled the kettle and switched it on.

"Tea?" Marcy raised her eyebrows.

I'd drunk it last time so couldn't really refuse, I didn't want her to think I was rejecting her or something. So I sat and patiently waited for the kettle to boil and for Marcy to hand me my steaming mug.

209

She sat at the kitchen table opposite me, just like before, hugging our mugs for security, not really knowing what to say.

"Mark said you found Rebecca," I managed at last.

Marcy smiled. "I'd finally got a job at Doncaster Royal Infirmary where I hoped to find out about you both. Over the twelve months I was there I made friends with people in different organisations. There was old information that you may be in Scarborough and that Rebecca may still be in Doncaster. But in the end I found her by accident. I was out walking one lunch break over Easter this year. It was such a warm sunny day. I walked up towards the nearby park and saw her. She was the image of me at that age, she couldn't be anyone else. I snapped a picture of her on my mobile then followed her down some steps onto the lower part of Armthorpe Road. I saw which house she went into and started making enquiries, making up different reasons for needing the information. Finally with the bits each one could tell me, it all tied in and I knew it was her." She shook her head. "But when I went to the house I was too late. The family had moved away. There was no forwarding address. I can't tell you how devastated I was. With the Doncaster leads gone I applied and managed to get a post here in Scarborough and the rest you know."

Marcy stared down at her drink. "Mark was never happy about the two of you. I guess I've always known that but tried to fool myself.

"I just wish he'd got me and not Gran," I said. "When he was at Gran's he told them everything. It was like he was convincing himself that he had only one option left, to get rid of me for good." I shivered.

"I just wish he'd talked to me at the beginning. I could've promised to stay out of his way or something."

"Then you would never have met me," Marcy said, softly.

I shrugged, unsure what to say.

"I'm sorry about what happened to your gran but I'm glad we met," she continued. Marcy slowly moved her cup around in circles on the table. "Are you sorry you met me?"

"No!" The word was out without me thinking about it. I clamped my mouth shut. Was I sorry? After all that'd happened did I wish I'd never known her? The thought spun around in my mind for a minute then I knew the answer. No, I was glad I'd met her. She was another part of me, a big part.

"No," I said, "I'm glad we met." Now it was my turn to look down. "Do you think, er, well, when I get home, er, do you think we could email each other or something?"

Marcy looked up at last, her face alight. She was like a child who'd just been promised a present. "You really want to?"

I nodded. "Yes. Now I've found you, well, now we've found each other, I don't want to lose you again."

"Oh, Rachel, you can't know how happy that makes me! I've worried about you both for years, wondering where you were, if you were okay. I've felt guilty the whole time, imagining all kinds of bad things happening to you. Wishing I'd had the courage to leave Jed before ... before giving you up. I'd love to keep in touch." She bit her lip. "Do you think, maybe, Rebecca ...?"

"Not right now, I asked her." I shrugged. "She might change her mind one day ..."

Marcy sighed. "I suppose I can't blame her, but maybe with you in touch with me, she might be curious someday?"

We talked for another hour and exchanged email addresses and mobile numbers. When I left we said 'goodbye' then sort of looked at each other. It was like we needed to do more than just say 'goodbye' but didn't know what we should do. In the end I reached out and gave her a hug, but then it felt so weird I let go real fast like I'd been burned. We both, sort of, looked at the floor, shuffling our feet. My cheeks were hot and when I looked up Marcy was blushing too.

"Well, bye," I said quickly. Flapping my arm in a quick wave, I headed down the street without looking back.

I didn't bother with a bus. It was a long walk to Gran's but I figured I needed time to get things straight in my head. I mean, having a birth mum I'd just met and trying to figure out how to relate to her was just so hard. I couldn't even bring myself to call her Mum. Janet Brooks was my mum, the one who'd brought me up all these years. The one who up to four months ago I actually thought *was* my birth mum.

And in one more week I'd be heading back to Rotherham. Back to Luke, Rebecca and my shy friend, Becca. Having only three people on my side and facing evil Emma and bullying Thompson was not exactly an exciting prospect.

By the time I got back to Gran's my feet were killing me and I was soaking wet and it wasn't from rain. The sun had come out mid walk and it was absolutely scorching! I shouted 'hello' to Mum and Gran and headed straight for the bath.

I lay in the warm refreshing water, my head still spinning. In the end I climbed out, wrapped a towel around me and just shrugged.

Worrying wasn't gonna make one minuscule bit of difference. I'd just have to take everything one day at a time. At least Gran'd be okay with Mum staying for as long as she needed.

***

My last week passed way too quickly, filled with sunbathing and laughing with my friends as well as spending every minute I could with Gran. On my last day I stood beside the coach and hugged Sapphire, Ruby, Summer and Sam. It was awful saying goodbye to them all again. This summer might have been a nightmare but I'd really enjoyed being back with my friends.

"See you on msn and facebook," Sam said with a strained smile.

"Yeah," I said, my eyes stinging. "Text you too."

"You'd better!" Sam wagged her finger at me, her head tipping from side to side in the usual bossy Sam look. "Or else."

"Ooh, I'm really scared!" I grinned.

"You'd better be, girl. And I want all the juicy gossip about Luke and the evil witches at school."

"Don't worry, I'll need somebody to sound off to and you're it!"

"Hey, don't forget us," Ruby piped up. "I mean, I got so many emails and texts last term I thought about getting a secretary."

I grimaced. "Yeah, sorry, I meant to write more, but like, it was pretty manic."

Ruby nodded sharply. "Yeah, well, you get let off just this once. Do better next time though Miss Brooks."

I grinned and saluted. "Yes ma'am, will do."

I turned to Mum and gave her a hug. "See you when you get home, Mum." I looked up at her. Our relationship hadn't been the same since finding out I was adopted but we were working on it. She'd always been there for me and that's what a real mum did. "I'll miss you," I said and meant it.

Mum smiled and wiped her eyes. "I'll miss you too, Sweetheart. I'll be back once your Gran's okay," she said and squeezed my shoulders.

"I can look after myself, I'll have you know." Gran pulled herself up to her full five foot two inches. "I don't need a baby sitter, I'm a big girl now."

Mum smiled down at her and I turned and wrapped my arms around her.

"I'm gonna miss you *soo* much, Gran." My eyes had stopped stinging now, they were wet instead as tears ran down my cheeks. "I *do* love you, Gran."

"I love you too, Sweetheart," my gran said, squeezing back. "And you are not to go worrying about me. I'll be fine." She leaned in closer and whispered in my ear. "Especially when I can get your mum to go home again, she fusses too much."

I pulled back and smiled through my tears. "Well, you take care, Gran and write to me okay?" I said, swiping the tears away with the back of my hand and taking deep breaths to stop more appearing.

"I'm not the one who doesn't do any writing or telephoning, now am I?" Gran wagged her finger at me and I grinned. This was my gran, the way she should be. I'd been so scared my feisty Gran was gone for good, all because of a coward who thought an old lady was an easy target. I was so glad Mark'd been caught, I just hoped he'd get sent away for a *looong* time.

"I'll write, Gran and phone this time. I promise."

Gran nodded and I knew I'd be in trouble if I didn't do as I said. Reluctantly I climbed onto the coach, dropping into the first available window seat. With my face close to the glass, I waved at my best friends and family. It would be a while before I saw them again. I waved even harder as the coach pulled out into traffic and they faded into the distance. Sitting back in my seat I closed my eyes, determined this time to write, text and email as promised.

But as the coach sped along the motorway and I watched the scenery slip by I was totally unaware that was one promise I wasn't gonna be able to keep...

Acknowledgements

Thank you to my proof readers Pam, Naomi and Christina for your constructive feedback, especially Christina for your teenage perspective. Also to Cornerstones Literary Consultancy for your editorial guidance.

I appreciate the help of Scarborough Tourist Information along with Chris Coombs and Rebecca Aspin from Scarborough Hospital who willingly provided all the local information I needed. Also Simon Dale and Steve Jones who gave up their time to take lots of photographs of Scarborough which made my job so much easier.

Thanks to my super sales reps – Mags Holdsworth and my dad! You did a fantastic job advertising 'Family Secrets'. Now that 'Family Fear' is out I have another task for you! Also to Waterstones, Philip Howard Books, Newstyme and Rotherham Libraries for supporting me. Along with Sandra Gabriel has been a great help providing lots of very useful contacts.

Thanks espccially to YouWriteOn.com without whom this book would not exist.

And lastly, but by no means least. Thanks to all those who read 'Family Secrets' and all your encouraging comments. You really make writing very worthwhile and I hope you enjoy 'Family Fear' just as much.

Watch out for:

Family Missing
By Gail Jones

Rebecca is missing. After a visit to her sister Rachel she never returns home.

The police launch a search for the missing twin, enlisting Rachel's help. But when Rachel agrees to do a reconstruction of Rebecca's last known steps, she has no idea how much danger she is placing herself in.

Can Rachel find and save Rebecca? Or will Rachel be the next one to go missing?

Family Missing
The third and final part of the Rachel Brooks trilogy

coming soon

To Keep up with all the latest news:

Visit Gail's website @

<u>www.gailjonesbooks.co.uk</u>

Or check out her facebook page @

Gail Jones Fiction UK

Lightning Source UK Ltd.
Milton Keynes UK
UKOW051036271011

181032UK00001B/25/P